Orphelia's World
Missouri in 1904

*Madame Meritta's
traveling show*

Calico
Creek

The Stone Shed

Mississippi River

St. Louis

1904 World's Fair

THE MINSTREL'S MELODY

❧

by
Eleanora E. Tate

American Girl ™
SCHOLASTIC INC.

New York Toronto London Auckland Sydney
Mexico City New Delhi Hong Kong Buenos Aires

ISBN 0-439-39062-1

12 11 10 9 8 7 6 5 4 3   2 3 4 5 6 7/0

Printed in the U.S.A.   23

First Scholastic printing, February 2002

Cover and Map Illustrations: Glenn Harrington
Line Art: Greg Dearth

To Evelyn Morgan, Merilyn Bruce Hamlett,
Gwendolyn Brooks, and Mary Carter Smith

TABLE OF CONTENTS

CHAPTER I

THE STONE SHED

Orphelia Bruce raised her hands to an imaginary piano keyboard and wiggled her slender fingers in the warm Missouri spring air.

"Pearl, are you ready now to sing?" she said over her shoulder to her older sister. "We have got to do better this time. Cap, I see you're ready on your, uh, drum." She glanced at the tall, light-skinned boy beside her, two sticks in his hands, beating on a schoolbook that swung on a strap around his neck. "All right! And one and two and three and four and—Pearl! You missed your cue again!"

Turning around, Orphelia saw Pearl bent over in the tall grass, examining the hem of her long muslin skirt. "I must have caught it on the fence back there," she said. "You know I can't sing in a raggedy skirt. So unprofessional. We got to call off practice."

"Girl, you're always tearing something." Orphelia tried

not to let her face frown up too much. "Come on, Pearl, we have got to rehearse. You're not getting up on that stage tomorrow night singing every which way with me and Cap."

"Oh? Well, maybe I just won't go at all." Pearl smiled wickedly. "Then we'll see who else'll get to be in Madame Meritta and Her Marvelous Traveling Troubadours Talent Show. How about that?"

Orphelia put her hands on her hips and opened her mouth, but Cap broke in. "You know your momma said if Pearl can't be in it, you can't either, so just be quiet, Orphelia. I'm not gonna look a fool banging out 'Listen to the Mockingbird' on a drum by myself."

"You mean banging on *my* book," Pearl said. "I don't think you got a real drum anyway. I bet you plan to fix up a sorghum bucket."

"Don't worry about my drum," Cap shot back. "You better worry more about getting another hole in your stocking."

"Did I? Where?" Pearl hitched up her skirt and examined her black cotton stockings.

Orphelia snatched at her sister's skirt. "Put your skirt down, you ninny! Look, I'll mend your hem good as new, all right? Stockings, too, if there's a hole. All right?"

Darn Pearl. So vain! Orphelia lifted her hands again to her pretend piano and tried to look as pitiful as she could at Pearl and Cap. "Now, please, please, please, please, *please* can we try it one more time?"

Pearl smiled at Cap, who turned red up and down his neck. She cleared her throat, patted her reddish brown hair upswept in a pompadour, and clasped her plump hands before her. She fluttered her long eyelashes and gazed into the sky. "All right. I'm ready. Proceed."

Pearl's raspy voice scraped out the opening words of "Listen to the Mockingbird." To help her stay in tune as much as possible, Orphelia added her own strong contralto voice. Good grumpety gracious, but Pearl was so off-key! She sang like that even when they practiced on the real piano at school.

And just where Cap was going to find a real drum in one day was something Orphelia told herself *not* to worry about. It was stupid to have a drum playing with them anyway, but that was another of Sister Pearl "Miss in Charge" Bruce's ideas. Orphelia had wanted a tambourine, but nobody she knew had one.

She sang louder to try to keep Pearl on key and tried not to wince when her sister hit another wrong note. Even though Pearl couldn't sing, Momma insisted that Pearl be part of Orphelia's performance. This was the price one paid to reach fame, Orphelia reminded herself.

Cap was not from around here. He'd dropped off of a train into their Calico Creek community a couple of months ago. He said he was twelve, but with that height and barrel chest, he looked a good fifteen or sixteen. Big old boy! Living by the Mississippi River in northeast

Missouri, in that corner where Missouri, Illinois, and Iowa came together, Orphelia had seen a lot of hobos who had passed through from steamboats, barges, and boxcars. The river and the railroad were natural highways for transients. She hadn't seen many as young as Cap, though.

The minute Cap saw Pearl, who was fourteen, he fell smack "in love" with her. Now he followed her around like somebody's pet goat.

Not that Orphelia minded much that boys seemed to like Pearl more, and that at first glance, folks told Orphelia to her face that Pearl was prettier than she was, and that Pearl was Momma's favorite. Well, she minded, but she refused to let any of it bother her, put it that way. Orphelia was rather pleased that her braided hair made her look dignified, that she was slender and athletic, and that Poppa said her chocolate skin, like his, was as smooth as a piece of fine furniture.

Best of all, she could sing and play piano better than anyone else in Lewis County, even including most of the adults. She was church pianist-in-training for their Calico Creek Missionary Baptist Church. She sang solo and played piano at all the school and church events. Once she even sang at the Emancipation Celebration way over in Hannibal. She had perfect pitch and practically a photographic memory, which meant that she could play any song after hearing or reading the music just once.

It stood to reason that she was going to be a star one day. Everybody said so. Well, Momma wouldn't say so. Momma would only say that Orphelia's voice was "sufficient" for religious music, that singing sassy songs was a sin, and that no daughter of hers would ever perform professionally onstage. She and Momma had had more than one fight about that.

"Mockingbir-r-r-r-d," Pearl shrieked, spreading her chubby arms. "Okay, I'm through. We don't need to sing more than two verses, anyway. C'mon, let's go home."

Orphelia sighed, dropped her hands, and followed Pearl down the road. Better this short practice than none at all. "Maybe we can come to school early tomorrow so we can use the piano," she said. Neither Pearl nor Cap answered.

"Remember, we can win first place, you all. Remember St. Louis and the World's Fair! Cap, ever been to St. Louis? Yes? No? We haven't, yet. But if—when—we win, we'll get to play during Madame Meritta's program at the Louisiana Purchase Exposition—the St. Louis World's Fair—next week! I love the sound of that. We'll be famous, you hear me? She's never brought her talent show to this part of Missouri before, Cap, so that must be a sign!"

"Orphelia, shut up. You're yapping so much I can't think," Pearl said.

Orphelia ignored the impulse to ask Pearl when did she ever think, and went on, "And maybe I could join up with Madame Meritta and Her Marvelous Traveling Troubadours show and travel all around the world. I'd wear furs and boas and diamond necklaces and sparkling dresses and a feather in my hat just like she does. Maybe I'd even get a beautiful gold tooth like she has. People would cram into her shows and swoon over me playing and singing. They'd throw money and roses at my feet."

"And when your daddy heard about it, he'd make them throw you out," Cap cracked.

"No, Poppa wouldn't," Pearl giggled, "but Momma would. Poppa'd just stand there and watch ol' skinny Orphelia go flying out through the tent door. Listen, Cap, when Momma's going to switch Orphelia, Poppa'll just go to the front porch or the outhouse and stay there until it's over."

"Oh have mercy heavens, Pearl, now *you're* the one flapping your lips," Orphelia said. She didn't want Cap to know that she still got switchings. "You keep falsifying like that and you'll give me heart palpitations. And I'm not skinny!"

"Kids from all over the state have been competing in that woman's talent shows for nearly a year," Cap reminded Orphelia. "This is her last stop anyway. She's probably already got the winner picked out, probably from Kansas City or Jeff City. She don't want no hicks around her. You and Clementine and Ambrose and anybody else from school who's gonna be in this thing's fooling yourselves. Don't even think about winning first place and going to St. Louis."

"You don't know that, so don't be so negative." Orphelia lifted her head and thrust out her chin. She picked her schoolbag up from the ground. Forget Cap.

As they walked past the Stone Shed, Orphelia stopped to scan the back-porch wall for new posters. The Stone Shed was a dilapidated old building set near the road, where people posted handbills, posters, broadsides, and other printed announcements. It wasn't actually made of stone but of wood. Everybody said it had been used once as a jail for colored people. But now it was like Calico Creek's community newspaper. And it was where, a whole year ago, Orphelia had first seen posters announcing the Louisiana Purchase Exposition—the World's Fair—starting April 30, 1904, in St. Louis.

Since then, news of the World's Fair had kept her thumbing through the newspapers that came to the school. Madame Meritta's poster, however, had appeared only a few weeks ago. The poster's announcement had made Orphelia almost faint with joy. The real Madame Meritta, coming to little Calico Creek, Missouri? Orphelia didn't care if Madame Meritta sang or not—if she could just *see* her! Well, if she *did* decide to sing, that would be even better. But it was a talent show for kids, after all.

For years Orphelia had read and saved as many newspaper clippings about Madame Meritta as she could find.

Madame Meritta was a star! She was born of free parents in 1864 in St. Louis and could play the piano at the age of four. By age seven she was known as "Little Miss Meritta, child prodigy." By the age of twelve—same age as Orphelia— she had run away from home and joined a minstrel show.

Once she was on the same program as John William "Blind" Boone, the famous Missouri piano player. Several times she performed with the renowned opera singers, the Hyers Sisters. Madame Meritta formed her own minstrel troupe, one of the very few Negro women to do so, and now she traveled around the world. She had her own customized coaches and everything. Her life sounded so exciting!

To see the great Madame Meritta in person would be a miracle in itself. To perform in her talent show was something Orphelia had only dreamed about and never thought possible. Until now.

This would be her first big break. One of these days she'd be so good that Momma would *have* to like all the music she played. She'd be so famous that her posters would be all over the Stone Shed. The *Hannibal Evening Courier* and the *Lewis County Journal* and even the St. Louis papers would have write-ups about her. One of these days, no matter what Momma said, Orphelia would be a minstrel star, too, just like Madame Meritta.

As Orphelia, Pearl, and Cap slowly began their long walk across the cow pasture for home, Mr. McCutcheon and his ice wagon, drawn by his cross-eyed mare Canola, rumbled past the Stone Shed. World's Fair posters were nailed to both sides of the wagon. Orphelia waved at him. If he had stopped at a customer's house, she and Pearl and Cap would have scrambled up to his wagon and gotten fresh, cool chunks of ice. Singing made her thirsty.

"Well, I know neither Poppa nor Momma's gonna ever let me or you sing sassy songs in public," Pearl was saying. "You know Momma says—"

"I know, I know! I have to hear it more than you do! 'Perform only proper music in public, sassy music and dancing are sinful, always sit with your ankles crossed, and always conduct yourselves as proper young Negro ladies, according to the standards of the day.' I am too tired of hearing that. Why Momma's so much against every kind of song I want to play except church music is what I can't understand. She's so old-fashioned. Why do she and Reverend Rutherford say dancing is sinful and will make your soul burn in the hereafter down below, but then won't tell you why?"

"Uh-oh, Orphelia's gone off again," Cap said. "Pearl, hold this chile down!"

Orphelia spread her arms wide and whirled around. "Shoot, this is 1904! People in Hannibal have motorcars and electric lights inside their houses. Miz Rutherford told us that two men flew in the air last year! I want to see the world. I wanna play ragtime, sing show tunes, do the cakewalk—c'mon, you all, let's high step!"

Breaking into a lively chorus of "Oh, Dem Golden Slippers," Orphelia grabbed Cap by the left arm and swung him around. Pearl grabbed his right arm. They strutted and high stepped about in the pasture like she'd seen folks do at the Emancipation Celebration.

Suddenly Pearl stopped. "I feel flushed," she panted. "Did Mr. McCutcheon see us dancing? Am I feeling the hot flames of the hereafter down below already?"

Orphelia laughed, but she stopped dancing, too, feeling guilty. How could something so enjoyable as music and dancing be a sin? Momma didn't want to talk about any kind of music unless it was church music. She didn't even want to talk about her own brother, Uncle Winston, who had played the cornet before he died. His picture hung in the hallway at home. He wore a band uniform and carried his cornet. A tiny silver pin shaped like a musical note sparkled on his lapel.

Momma would only say that Uncle Winston died when he was a young man, that his cornet playing was "sufficient," and that Orphelia should let his soul rest in peace. Poppa was as closemouthed as a clam about him, too. Orphelia couldn't even pry anything out of Miz Rutherford. Orphelia felt a connection with him, as he seemed to have been the only other instrumentalist in the family.

Just then Pearl nudged her. "There must be something to what Reverend said. Dancing's put Cap on the road to sin already. Look!" Cap had trotted along the dirt path to the porch of the old Stone Shed and was removing boards that were loosely nailed across the door.

"Get away from there!" Orphelia yelled. "Sheriff Lasswell owns all this, and I personally heard him say he'd arrest anybody who fools around in this building. Can't you read that 'Keep Out' sign? Ain't nothing in there for you. Cap, you hear me?"

Without answering, Cap pushed his way into the Shed. "Well, I declare," said Pearl. "Where he comes from, trespassing must not be against the law. I suppose he figures he can do anything, being a man, or near big as one."

Cap reappeared in the door with a drum in his hands. "Told you I had a drum. I know what I'm talking about. Come see what all's in here. Pearl, come look."

"Don't you do it," Orphelia said.

But Pearl hotfooted along the path to the porch. She peeked in the door. "Where'd you steal this drum? Cap, I'm not getting in trouble over your—oh, my goodness gracious! Looka-here! Orphelia, you got to come see!" Then she disappeared through the door, too.

"Momma's gonna skin you and fry you up for going in there," Orphelia warned. She folded and unfolded her arms, dying to go in, too. If this place used to be a jail, why would a drum be in there?

"Pearl, you come out here right now!" She took a step forward on the path and stopped, then took a few steps more. She swatted at a grasshopper that jumped from a stand of Queen Anne's lace onto her blouse. "Better come out before you give me heart palpitations!"

Cautiously she stepped onto the creaky porch and peeked in. Cap and Pearl stood in the middle of a large, dusty, spiderweb-strewn room. Sunlight through the cracks in the roof and walls gave her just enough light to see large piles of newspapers and rags on the floor, wooden straight-back chairs, a divan, a fireplace, a magnificent iron chandelier, and massive wood tables with legs the size of pillars. The air smelled like wet, decaying tree bark and rotted leaves.

Pearl and Cap pointed to a corner of the room where against the wall sat—an upright piano! The only other pianos Orphelia knew to be in the Calico Creek community were in their church and school. Eyes riveted to the instrument, Orphelia dashed into the room. She lifted the dusty piano lid and touched a few keys. Tinny sounds came out. Already she loved it.

"Shoosh, thing needs tuning bad," she said. "But I sure wish I could take it home! It needs somebody like me to take care of it."

Cap proudly set the drum back up on top of the piano. "Ain't this the funniest looking 'jail' you ever saw?"

"Looks more like it was a dance hall or a saloon, or a

music room." Orphelia ran her fingers over the keys again. "But not a jail! Why would the sheriff and everybody tell us such things?"

"To keep nosy little children like you out of here," said Cap.

"Oh yeah? Well, what does that make *you*? And how'd you know about that drum being in here anyway?" Orphelia asked. She played a few more notes, wondering if Reverend Rutherford could tune pianos.

"'Cause I bet he's been in here before," Pearl said. "Tore those boards off like they were matchsticks, just like that, strong as you are." She plucked his shirt sleeve flirtatiously.

Cap puffed out his chest and hooked his thumbs into his belt. "When you travel around like me, you got to know how to do. Otherwise you be sleeping in the mud with the pigs and cows. We fellas on the road spot out places like this and tell each other. After I got kicked off—hopped off the train, I remembered a fella telling me about an old building out in the country. He described it perfectly, so I came right to it. A rug makes a good blanket when you ain't got nothing else, and a floor beats sleeping on the ground anytime."

Orphelia wandered around the room, still puzzling over their discovery. Would Sheriff Lasswell be sinful enough to have a saloon? He surely didn't seem so musically inclined as to have a formal music room. She picked up some newspapers from a pile on the floor. Most were dusty, moldy, and crumbling. Sneezing, she went through the pile quickly. She returned to the piano and picked up a torn, faded handbill of two young men next to a young woman sitting at a piano.

She showed the handbill to Pearl, who was examining a swatch of brocaded material on the floor. "Wonder who they were," Orphelia said.

Pearl glanced at the handbill, then picked up and fondled the cloth. "Wouldn't this make a grand spread on my bed? If I slip this in our room, would you keep your mouth shut?"

Orphelia laughed. "Like Momma wouldn't notice a strange, moldy, yellow, red, and green piece of cloth on your bed and not have a hissy fit. If I can't take the piano, you can't take that cloth."

"I'll wait for a good time, like when she's busy, and tell Momma I found this old rag by the road and could I wash it and make it nice. She won't be listening that close, anyway. I want that piece of paper with those people, too. I can hang it on the wall. I'll say, 'Why, Momma, where'd this handbill come from? It must have been stuck to this cloth!'" Winking at Orphelia, Pearl took the handbill. She folded the cloth and slid the handbill between the layers.

"Who would have thought the Stone Shed held anything but dust?" Orphelia turned to Cap. "According to Miz Rutherford, this house was once owned by a white family named Stone. That's why they call it the Stone Shed, you know, even though it's made out of wood. Anyway, Miz Rutherford said it was where runaway slaves hid out, called an Underground Railroad or something. Being so close to Illinois, they would cross the Mississippi and go over to Quincy and be free. Or else they went on to towns in Iowa like Salem, Denmark, or Burlington and were free there."

"You talkin' like we're in school," Cap said. "What I figure is that the sheriff ended up with it and used to have dances and stuff out here. The grown folks knew what it really was, but they called it a jail and you all believed it. That's why you all been so scared to come inside. You can't be that green to believe everything grown folks say, can you?"

"Yes," Pearl broke in before Orphelia could speak. "We better get out of here before someone else comes around. Orphelia, I just thought of something. Today's the day we do Sheriff Lasswell's clothes."

Momma was the best laundress in town, and she washed and ironed the clothes of the most prosperous white families around. Pearl and Orphelia usually helped. "That must be a sign that it's all right for me to take this piece of cloth. I'm just doing more of his clothes!" Pearl patted her skirt. It bulged out more than usual.

"Cap, you're a witness that I didn't have anything to do with Pearl stealing that cloth. So, Pearl, don't put me into your falsifying." Orphelia returned to the piano. She wished she could put *it* under her skirt.

She started to sit down at the piano when she noticed paper sticking out from under the piano-bench lid. Lifting up the lid, she found more sheet music and a small composition book. Reading sheet music was how she learned many songs, apart from those she heard played at functions or that Miz Rutherford gave her in music books. Orphelia broke into a smile as she thumbed through the pages of the composition book. Written on the cover were the words "Songbook" and "Private" in a fine hand. The book contained several pages of musical compositions. One song was entitled "Lewis County Rag." She'd never heard that one before. Ignoring the privacy notice, Orphelia squinted at the notes and began to play. It was the same kind of music that man Scott Joplin down in Sedalia was getting famous for creating. She played the entire song.

"Orphelia! Get off that piano and come on!" Pearl called from the door. "Else I'm leaving you in here by yourself."

Orphelia stuffed the little book into her bodice. She couldn't wait to get to school and play the song when Miz Rutherford wasn't around. Whose book was this, and why had it been left behind? Whose instruments were these? And what had this room and this building really been used for after the Stone family left?

CHAPTER 2

PUNISHED

 ap left them at the crossroads.
When Orphelia and Pearl reached
their yard, they saw Momma in the back
taking down Sheriff Lasswell's red flan-
nel long underwear from the line. They
slipped into the house. While Pearl
paused in the kitchen, Orphelia eased
into the bedroom she and Pearl shared.
She removed the songbook from her bodice and hid it
under the cover of her bed to examine later.

As she changed from her school dress into a plain skirt
and waist, Pearl came in smiling and chewing on a piece
of johnnycake. "I just put that cloth in a laundry basket.
Momma'll never know the difference." Pearl changed her
clothes, too, and then they left the room.

Orphelia was glad to notice Poppa's blue-and-white-
striped work coat hanging in the hallway. It meant he
was home for now and not traveling up and down the
Missouri Railroad line, repairing the rails. Poppa's job

with the railroad as a gandy dancer was a good one, but it kept him away a lot.

Back outside, Momma glanced at Orphelia but smiled brightly at Pearl. "Take that basket in and start ironing," she told Pearl. "You be careful you don't catch yourself on fire around the stove or burn yourself on the iron. Orphelia, start taking those clothes down off the line. And don't drop anything. You know how clumsy you are."

As clumsy as Pearl is, Momma better watch that she *doesn't scorch Mrs. Lasswell's petticoats,* Orphelia thought. Aloud she said, "Momma, you should have heard us practicing this afternoon. Pearl was just singing and singing, and I was on my pretend piano. We're gonna sound great tomorrow night."

"You'd do better to practice for Sunday morning service," Momma replied over the hot tub of lye soap.

At dinner Pearl jabbered away about school like she was the only one in it. *Girl has a mouth that runs like one of those autocars,* Orphelia thought. She drummed her fingers on the table. When she failed to get Momma's attention, she waved at Poppa.

"Stop that," Momma said. "Wait your turn to speak."

And what day would that be? Orphelia wanted to say, but she knew better.

Poppa saw the look on her face. "And how was your day today, Li'l Sweets?" Poppa said, using his nickname for her.

"We practiced our act on the way home, with Cap banging on Pearl's schoolbook for a drum. He said he has a real drum, though. May I go to school early tomorrow and practice on the piano?"

"And, Poppa, Cap and us was walking by the Stone Shed," Pearl blabbered, "and Cap went in and—"

"What?" Momma and Poppa said together.

Pearl shut up. She lowered her eyes and concentrated on her wieners and sauerkraut. Orphelia thought fast. "Momma, you need any more help with the laundry tonight?"

"Cap did what?" Momma ignored Orphelia. "What? Pearl, I'm waiting for you to tell me more about Cap and the Shed."

"Nothing," said Pearl.

"But you two know better than to go in, don't you?" Poppa said. "Pearl? You stayed put, didn't you? Didn't you? Pearl?"

Momma said in her cold, quiet "switching time" voice, "Pearl Charise Bruce, did you go into the Shed?"

Eyes still cast down at her plate, Pearl shook her head no ten times, fast. She looked up, from Poppa to Momma to Orphelia, who was holding her breath. Then Pearl nodded her head yes slowly, once. "But, Momma, Orphelia went in, too."

Orphelia's mouth fell open. "Pearl!"

"Against our word?" Momma turned to Orphelia.

"But, Momma, it was Pearl's fault! Cap went in and called to Pearl, Pearl went in and called to me, but I kept telling them both not to go in!" Orphelia said. Goose bumps popped out on her arms. Her braids felt tight.

"I am so disappointed in you, Orphelia. You go off and do these things and don't care what we say." Momma's normally pale brown face was flushed an angry red. "What were you thinking, to go following after some boy and trespass on the sheriff's property?"

Orphelia kept quiet. Momma never could admit that Pearl ever did anything wrong. It was like Momma suddenly sprouted horse blinders when it came to Pearl. *Sure must be nice to be the favorite.*

"And what happened after you got in?" Poppa was saying to Pearl. "Tell me the truth."

"I saw a bunch of papers and junk. I came right back out. I kept calling to Orphelia to come out, too, but she stayed. So I went back in to get her. She had this piece of paper with two men and a lady on it and showed it to me. I told her to put it down and I made her come out. Honest."

"Poppa, she's lying again! Momma, I—"

"You hush up right now, Orphelia!" Momma said. Her gray eyes had turned to the color of cold steel. "Don't you ever say that word 'lying' ever again. I didn't

raise girls to use such crude language or to disobey me.
Where's that piece of paper? Orphelia, show it to me
this minute!"

"I don't have it. Pearl was the one who took it!"

"I know where she put it, Momma. I'll get it." Pearl
jumped up from the table and ran into their bedroom.

Had Pearl seen her hide the songbook? *Oh Lord, how
did I get caught up in another one of Pearl's lies this time?*
thought Orphelia.

"I just don't know what gets into you!" Momma
fumed. "Orphelia, you're so bullheaded. You just think
you can do whatever you want. Well, take your soul to
Jesus because your *behind* is *mine*."

"But that's not fair!" Orphelia cried. "You ought to
switch Pearl, too!"

"You best worry about your own self right now,"
Momma snapped.

Pearl trooped back into the kitchen with Orphelia's
schoolbag. "Look! See?" She jerked the faded handbill
from the schoolbag and gave it to Momma. Staring at
it, Momma went pale. She gaped at Orphelia like she'd
seen a ghost.

Orphelia snatched her bag from Pearl. "You leave
my stuff alone! Momma, Poppa, Pearl put that in my bag.
I asked her who the people were, and she said she was
gonna sneak it home—"

"Be quiet." Poppa took the handbill from Momma

and studied it. Slowly he tore it into pieces and dropped the pieces on top of the sauerkraut on his plate.

"Why won't you tell them the truth?" Orphelia hollered at Pearl. "And what did you do with that piece of cloth you stole from there and stuck up under your skirt?"

"What piece of cloth?" asked Poppa. "Pearl, did you—"

"We're not discussing Pearl or any cloth right now," said Momma in that icy, quiet voice. "Orphelia, I don't think I'll switch you."

Orphelia stared at her, not knowing what to say. It wasn't like Momma to change her mind so quick like that. Should Orphelia thank her? On the other hand, as awful as a switching was, maybe it would be better than whatever else Momma might have in mind.

When Momma switched her, she'd make Orphelia go out in the front yard and cut a branch from the weeping willow tree to use. Orphelia would always find the smallest twig she could. Sometimes she had to go back out several times until she brought in one that satisfied Momma. Then she had to strip off its leaves and take off her skirt and stockings. Clementine Madison said her Momma did it the same way. Orphelia hated that weeping willow tree.

Orphelia ate the rest of her dinner in silence. So did Momma, Poppa, and Pearl. No one mentioned Pearl's stolen cloth. Momma had spoken, and there was nothing more to say. But if Momma wasn't going to switch

Orphelia, what *would* she do? It was just like Momma to make Orphelia wait for a punishment. How long would she have to wait this time?

Orphelia wondered and waited while she and Pearl collected the dirty dishes. Poppa stood up and left the kitchen. Orphelia followed him with her eyes, wishing he would stay. She and Pearl silently washed and dried the dishes. The sun disappeared behind a bank of thick purple storm clouds. Lightning flashed among them. A storm was on its way.

After finishing up the dishes, Orphelia waited for Momma's storm to break, too. She felt like she'd pop if she had to wait any longer. But when Momma removed her apron and finally turned to Orphelia, she jumped.

"No, this time I won't switch you," Momma said, folding her arms. "But you can just forget about being in that talent show."

Orphelia's face stung like Momma had slapped her. "No, no! Momma, oh please—don't take me out, please! Switch me, I don't care, but not the talent show!"

"That's what I said and that's what I mean."

"Momma, please!" Orphelia rushed out of the kitchen, her hands to her head. She ran through the hallway, past the portrait of Uncle Winston, and found Poppa sitting at his desk reading the newspaper. "Poppa, Momma said I can't be in the show! Poppa, that's not fair! Don't let her take me out of the show!"

Without looking up, he said, "You buttered your bread, now eat it. Maybe you'll think twice next time before disobeying us."

Orphelia flung the dish towel onto the floor. She stamped off to her room and threw herself across the bed, too angry to cry. She wished she could die. All because of Pearl, Pearl, Pearl! *Big-mouth liar, lying to save her own behind!* Calling somebody a liar was fighting words, but she didn't care about that. How could Momma and Poppa believe Pearl's lies all the time? How could they be so mean? They knew how much the talent show meant to Orphelia. And couldn't Poppa have taken her side just this once?

When Pearl edged into the room, Orphelia sat up, her fists clenched and her heart pounding. "You double-crossing, mealy-mouthed, low-down lying sow!"

Pearl stayed by the door and kept her hand on the leather drawstring that served as a knob. "It just slipped out. I didn't mean to. I didn't want to be in that ol' show, anyway. There's always some ol' program coming up where you can show off. I get tired of having to hear people always bragging on you. You think you're so great, ol' ugly, skinny thing!"

"And you're a selfish, jealous, lying pig! Pretty on the outside and so ugly on the in!"

"You keep calling me names and I'll tell Momma that—that—you were dancing! Flirting and twisting your behind and kicking up your legs with a boy around. And whistling, too!"

"So were you!" But Pearl would be crazy enough to lie to Momma about that, too. Flirting and whistling around boys were just as bad a sin as playing sassy music and dancing. Orphelia lay back down and turned away from Pearl. She listened to her thumping heart.

"I can't stand it when Momma gets mad at me," Pearl said. "She gets mad at you so much you should be used to it."

"She never gets mad at you for anything. But I know one thing. I know that you're gonna burn in the hereafter down below for all those lies. Every inch of your fat's gonna sizzle and pop and drip grease down on the rest of us."

Orphelia heard the other bed creak as Pearl sat down on it. *She's thinking that last part over,* Orphelia told herself. *I wish I could have thought of that to say to her while we were at the dinner table. Momma really would have had a fit then!*

"Lord knows I don't want to burn in the hereafter down below," Pearl finally said. "I didn't mean to say those things. I'm really sorry about the talent show. I didn't think Momma'd get so mad she'd pull us out. I'll make it up to you, I promise. But I can't go back in there and change what I said, not now. She'd just get madder. Say you'll forgive me, Orphelia. I promise I'll make it up to you."

"But that's the only way I *can* forgive you—if you tell

Momma the truth right now. Then maybe she'll change her mind before it's too late and put me back in the show."

"Well, I can't. Maybe later. I said I'd make it up to you. Now I don't want to talk about it anymore." Pearl turned down the light in the kerosene lamp on the nightstand between their beds and pulled the covers to her chin.

Orphelia watched the light flicker on the wall for several minutes as she went over and over this awful turn of events. She stared at the flowery wallpaper in the dim light. Finally she fought back the ache in her heart the only way she knew how. Playing her favorite songs on her imaginary piano, she pretended that the flowers on the wall were people's faces—the faces of her audiences in Kansas City, St. Louis, Memphis, Sedalia, Chicago, New Orleans, London, Paris, Spain, China, all around the world. "Lewis County Rag" came to her mind. Each note rang out as clearly in her brain as when she had played the song on the out-of-tune piano that afternoon.

By the end of her mental recital, Orphelia's spirits had risen a little, but only a very little.

As Orphelia whispered her evening prayers, the tears finally came. "Oh when, dear Lord, will I ever have another chance to play for the famous Madame Meritta? And why, oh Lord, does Momma hate the music that I love so much, and why does she seem to hate me, too?"

Early the next morning before school began, Orphelia, with swollen red eyes, stood silently and miserably by Miz Rutherford's desk while Pearl told their teacher that they couldn't be in the talent show.

"Well, I declare!" Miz Rutherford said after Pearl finished. "On the day of the talent show, why in the world would your momma suddenly think it lacks moral uplift?"

She stood up from her desk and came around to Orphelia. She placed one hand on Orphelia's left shoulder, lifted up her chin with the other hand, and looked deeply into her puffy eyes. Orphelia could smell peppermint on her breath.

"Do you want me to talk with your momma and see if she'll change her mind?" Miz Rutherford asked. "I assured all the parents from the start that Madame Meritta conducts very proper, Christian talent shows. After all, it's being sponsored by the church! My goodness, it's even being held on church grounds."

Orphelia wished she could tell her teacher that "moral uplift" had nothing to do with their withdrawal. But aloud she only said, "It wouldn't make any difference. You know Momma." Leaving Pearl and Miz Rutherford, she walked outside to where Demetria and Clementine Madison and Panella Dade stood on the steps, listening through the half-open door.

"I didn't think your momma was *that* strict," said Demetria.

"Your momma decided she didn't want to get embarrassed from having everybody hear Pearl onstage mooing like a cow, didn't she?" said Panella. "Too bad for you, better for us." She and her sister were in the show and would recite and act out two poems by the famous poet Paul Laurence Dunbar.

Orphelia tightened her lips but kept quiet.

"Look there," said Clementine, "see how Orphelia's face got all scrunched up just then? Pearl had something to do with it for sure, like always. Excuse us, please! I got to talk to this girl!"

Orphelia let Clementine, a tall, thin, brown-skinned, pigeon-toed girl with moles on her face, take her arm. Silently they walked over to the hollyhocks, away from the other girls. In tonight's talent show Clementine was going to give an interpretive dance to "Swing Low, Sweet Chariot" while her younger brother Ambrose played the song on his cornet. Orphelia had always wondered why Clementine didn't dance pigeon-toed like she walked.

"All right, what'd Pearl do this time?" asked Clementine. "You look like you're gonna bust out bawling. Seems like Pearl's always doing some kind of devilishness to take the strut out of your step."

"Pearl had something to do with it," Orphelia said, "but not like what you think." She usually felt safe sharing her problems with Clementine. This time, though, telling Clementine that they had been in the Stone Shed would bring up more questions and might even lead to bigger problems if the wrong grown-ups found out.

Orphelia breathed in deep and blew out her breath hard. "I'm so mad at Momma and Pearl I could spit fire! I was so mad last night that I called Pearl a liar to her face, and Momma about had a hissy fit. But at least she's letting me come to watch the show tonight. Maybe Madame Meritta will sign my program and give me her address and let me write to her."

"But what did Pearl do?"

"Doesn't matter. It's done now."

"All right, then don't tell me." For a moment Clementine sounded hurt. "Well, maybe Madame Meritta will have another talent show come through next year, and you can try then."

Miz Rutherford came to the school door and began ringing her handbell, signaling the start of school. Orphelia freed her arm from Clementine's.

"I'm not waiting until next year. I don't know exactly when and I don't know what, but I'm gonna do something about this—soon. You just watch me, Clementine."

CHAPTER 3
MARVELOUS MADAME MERITTA

 From a distance, Orphelia could see that Calico Creek's church and school yard were already crowded with people. It was barely six o'clock in the evening, and most of the pews and chairs brought outside from the church were full. The talent show was not scheduled to start until six-thirty.

The stage—a platform of boards assembled by Reverend Rutherford, pastor of Calico Creek Missionary Baptist Church and Miz Rutherford's husband—was at one side of the building. On the stage sat a trio of musicians on banjo, drums, and piano. They began playing "Jesus Loves Me," and Orphelia hummed along.

"Slow down and walk ladylike, Orphelia," Momma called out behind her. "And straighten your bonnet before it slips off your head."

Orphelia slowed down a little without answering. She didn't care if the bonnet fell completely off and got trampled in the dust. Having to wear a hot bonnet was like having to wear a padlock around her head. And being forced out of the talent show was like having a padlock around her heart.

As she neared the yard she saw boys and girls wearing their best suits and dresses, carrying musical instruments and recital books. A boy she didn't recognize wore a gray beard and a top hat. She guessed he was portraying Abraham Lincoln and would recite the Emancipation Proclamation or the Gettysburg Address. Somebody usually did in programs like these.

When they found seats in a pew near the back of the seating section, Orphelia made sure to settle herself on the end by Poppa, with Momma and Pearl on the other side of him. That way she wouldn't have to hear much of Momma's criticisms of the show, or listen to Pearl's chatter. Orphelia had hardly said a word to either one of them since last night.

She patted sweat off her face with her bonnet strap and strained to see around the people sitting in front of her.

Behind the stage, school, and church, Orphelia spied three horse-drawn wooden coaches painted blazing red and yellow. Written on each coach in black curlicue lettering was "Madame Meritta and Her Marvelous Traveling Troubadours." Horses? No motorcar or rail? All of the newspaper stories Orphelia had read said that the entertainer had private railroad cars for her troupe of twenty musicians and assistants to eat and sleep in.

Miz Rutherford stood by one of the coaches, talking to a tall, pretty, dark-skinned woman in a plain brown dress. That couldn't be Madame Meritta, could it? Where were her boas and fancy gowns? Where was the rest of her show?

Momma was wondering the same thing. "Is that all there is?" she asked Poppa. "The way some folks talk, you'd think this woman's foot never touched the ground. Where's all these fine musicians she's supposed to have?"

A man in the next pew turned around and frowned a little at Momma. He pointed to the stage. "She has a huge entourage and a string of boxcars—I've seen 'em—but they say she's sent most of them on to St. Louis to get ready for the fair. I doubt if *she'll* perform tonight. It's a talent show for the kids, remember?"

Momma said, "Oh," and sniffed.

Orphelia looked around for Clementine. She was standing by the stage with the other competitors, including the boy in the Lincoln clothes. He had removed his top hat and was fanning himself with it. A boy who had supposedly rode his pet mule all the way from Canton with a big cello was drinking water. She didn't see Cap. When she had told him this morning that they'd been withdrawn, he'd just shrugged and said that Pearl needed to control her mouth better.

A barefoot boy in a straw hat and denim overalls held

a paintbrush and bucket. Orphelia figured he was portraying a character from one of the books by that Hannibal writer, Mark Twain.

Momma had forbidden Orphelia and Pearl to read any of the man's books because she said the language in his books was not morally uplifting. But one night when Orphelia had slept over at Clementine's, they had read several chapters of one of his books that had been serialized in the Hannibal newspaper. The story did have disgusting words in it. Other parts were funny. Orphelia and Clementine wondered if that man Jim in the book ever got free.

Orphelia recognized two girls in matching green dresses and pompadour hairstyles, plucking violins. They had participated in Hannibal's Emancipation Celebration festivities, billing themselves as "The Hannibal Twins, Prodigies on Violins."

The audience included white people, too. Orphelia didn't recognize a lot of people. They must have been from outside the county.

Miz Rutherford stepped upon the platform and rang her school bell for silence. "Ladies and gentlemen and little gentlemen and little ladies. What a momentous occasion it is for us to be so very privileged to have among us the marvelous Madame Meritta of St. Louis, Missouri. Madame Meritta, as you know, is the owner of Madame Meritta's Marvelous Traveling Troubadours.

She is here with us tonight seeking Missouri's most talented young artists. Of course, she'll find them right here in Lewis County, won't she?"

Everybody applauded. Some of the boys stamped their feet and whistled. Miz Rutherford went on. "Madame Meritta has traveled and performed around the world and before all of the royal families of Europe. She is among Missouri's most popular Negro musicians and is one of the state's and country's few minstrel show owners of feminine persuasion. We thank her deeply for giving of her precious time to visit our humble county and to give our children an opportunity to exhibit their talents here tonight."

Miz Rutherford went on talking like that until Orphelia wanted to shout, "Please, please, please get on with the show!"

Finally she left the stage. Orphelia leaned forward in anticipation. Then Reverend Rutherford came on and asked them to close their eyes and bow their heads. He offered up a prayer thanking God for bringing Madame Meritta to their school and church, and he asked God to continue to watch over everybody and to give special guidance to the young competitors who represented the cream of Lewis County.

Or most of it, Orphelia whispered to herself. The pain of being left out twisted at her heart.

As soon as he said amen, people around her gasped and began to applaud. Orphelia opened her eyes. Standing on the platform was the famous Madame Meritta at last. She wore a sleeveless turquoise silk gown, covered with a sparkly goldlike dust. A filmy white shawl lay lightly around her shoulders and hung down to the floor. On her head was a turquoise turban, one tail of which trailed down her right cheek. The turban was highlighted by a gold feather that also sparkled in the early evening sun. A diamond necklace twinkled at her throat. She lifted one arm—covered by a golden glove up to her elbow— and waved and smiled. When she smiled, Orphelia saw that her two front teeth were gold, too.

Poppa nudged Orphelia. "Close your mouth, girl! You'll let in flies," he said, smiling.

"Oh, Poppa, she's beautiful," Orphelia whispered. She stood up and waved back until Momma tapped her on the arm.

Without speaking, Madame Meritta floated across the platform to a white-draped table and sat down at it. As she did, a man in a white formal suit and derby strode out onto the stage.

"That's Mr. Interlocutor from her show," the man in front of Orphelia whispered to everybody. "Every minstrel show has someone they call Mr. Interlocutor. He plays the main man in charge of everything, and other performers tease and poke fun at him during the show. It's part of their act."

The man on stage, however, announced that he was

the Grand Master Roberts, master of ceremonies.
Orphelia wondered what the difference was between
Grand Master and Mr. Interlocutor.

Grand Master Roberts sang the praises of Madame
Meritta and the Rutherfords and then announced the
prizes to be given out. Third prize was a large framed
portrait of Madame Meritta with her signature, which
he held up.

"I wouldn't mind having one of those," Orphelia
told Poppa.

Second place was a trophy to be engraved with the
winner's name. First place, of course, meant that you
advanced to the finals and would appear with the other
winners during the entertainer's performance at the
St. Louis World's Fair next Saturday. The show was only
a little over a week away!

Orphelia joined the rest of the audience in clapping,
but her heart was not in it. Darn that Pearl and her big
mouth!

The acts were called and the children performed.
After reciting the Emancipation Proclamation, the boy
playing Abe Lincoln dropped his top hat when he bowed.
The Hannibal Twins, however, were perfect in their
rendition of "Flight of the Bumblebee," one of Orphelia's
favorite pieces, too. But she didn't need the music to
play it, like they did. "They'll be hard to beat tonight,"
she said to Poppa.

"You could have beat them," Poppa whispered back.

"Really?" Orphelia smiled wider than she had since Momma's devastating words the night before. Then she frowned. "But why didn't you say something to Momma?"

"I did."

She looked up at him, but Poppa kept his eyes on the stage. She sighed. She wiggled her fingers, which itched to play, then pressed them down in her lap.

At intermission, Orphelia slipped away from Momma and Pearl and stepped inside the church. The outside sounds of the trio music and of people talking and laughing were muffled in the cool solitude of the sanctuary. Orphelia went over to her old friend the church piano and sat down. She pulled off her bonnet and dropped it on the floor.

She began softly with "Amazing Grace," one of her favorite religious songs, and followed it with "Listen to the Mockingbird." When she was not struck down by God for singing a secular song in church—again—she moved into "Drink to Me Only with Thine Eyes," her mind and fingers finding comfort in the touch of the keys and the sound of her own voice.

Orphelia knew she could have won the talent show and gone on to perform at the St. Louis World's Fair, but now nobody would ever know.

"You sing and play superbly," said a strange voice behind her.

Orphelia jumped off the piano stool, her heart pounding. Her mouth went as dry as a dirt road. She pressed her hands to her chest. Madame Meritta!

"I was showing Madame Meritta around and she heard the piano," Miz Rutherford said, beaming. "I knew it could have been only you. Madame Meritta, this is my little star, Orphelia Bruce. Orphelia has been an admirer of yours for quite some time."

Madame Meritta held out her golden-gloved hand. Orphelia stared at it until Miz Rutherford cleared her throat. Taking a deep breath, Orphelia took the entertainer's hand in both of hers and shook it vigorously.

"I am Orphelia Bruce," she said slowly, "and I have the ut-ut-utmost pleasure of . . . of making your acquaintance. And I thank you for honoring us with . . . with your presence. I love your music and you're so beautiful and I want to be just like you," she finished in a rush. "And I hope you won't get mad because I was playing secular music in church, Miz Rutherford."

"As if it was the first time?" Miz Rutherford was still smiling. "Madame Meritta, Orphelia wants to sing and perform professionally. But we'd like for her to stay right here with us forever."

"Orphelia, your voice is beautiful. Why aren't you in the talent show?"

When Orphelia hesitated, Miz Rutherford spoke up. "Family reasons."

"Miz Madame, I love brass band music, and musical theater and minstrel shows, and of course religious music, and I'm so glad you don't sing songs that make fun of colored folks and you don't blacken up your face with burnt cork like those other minstrel groups do." She made herself stop and take a breath.

"Thank you. I've always thought it was degrading to smear that stuff on our faces when we were already Negro. You are exactly the kind of musician that I would love to have in my show. Such passion!" Gently pulling her hand from Orphelia's, she turned to Miz Rutherford. "She's so much more talented than any child in my talent shows so far."

"Yes, yes, yes!" Orphelia jumped and clapped her hands, then pressed them over her heart. *Oh, Lord, you heard my prayers!* "Would you tell this to my mother and father?"

"Let's wait until after the show," Miz Rutherford said. "Intermission's nearly over, and Madame Meritta needs to get back to judging. Isn't this wonderful, Orphelia? You wanted to meet her, and you have! The Lord works in mysterious ways."

Orphelia proudly led Miz Rutherford and Madame Meritta from the church into the throngs of people, noting that everybody—especially Momma and Pearl, Clementine, and the Hannibal Twins—was staring at them. "And be sure and tell your mother that I brought

Madame Meritta to *you*," Miz Rutherford whispered.
"I don't want you to get in trouble." Orphelia nodded.

She made her way back to their pew. "Miz Rutherford
introduced me to Madame Meritta, and she wants to meet
you and Poppa," she told Momma.

"Now isn't that nice," said Poppa. Momma just said,
"Hmmmm."

Orphelia hardly noticed the rest of the show. After
it ended, Madame Meritta deliberated, and Grand Master
Roberts announced the winners. Clementine and Ambrose
won third place, and the cellist won second. They all came
up onstage when their names were called and received
their prizes from Madame Meritta.

First place, as Orphelia had expected, went to the
Hannibal Twins. Madame Meritta gave them an envelope
and whispered something in their ears. Then she asked the
parents of all of the participants to stand, and they did.

Madame Meritta walked to the front of the stage.
"In the course of my visit here, I happened to hear a truly
gifted young lady sing, and I was so impressed with her
magnificent voice and piano playing that I must find some
way to acknowledge her. You all have heard her perform
before in the area. Her name is . . ." and she hesitated,
turning to Miz Rutherford.

Momma reached across Pearl and Poppa and tapped
Orphelia on the arm. "What's going on here?" she whispered sharply.

"I don't know," Orphelia said, her fingers intertwined in her lap.

"Her name is Orphelia Bruce," Madame Meritta continued. "Would you please stand, Miss Bruce, so that the audience can see you? Let's show her our appreciation for her talents with a round of applause."

Not daring to look at Momma's face, Orphelia stood up and then shot back down. She bit nervously on her thumb. A chance to go to the fair still?

"Orphelia, I said what is this all about?" Momma demanded, but Poppa motioned to her to be quiet. Orphelia looked up at Poppa in surprised gratitude. She stole a glance at Momma. Momma was eyeing her with a strange, almost frightened expression on her face. What would happen now?

Almost as soon as the show ended, Miz Rutherford steered Madame Meritta through the crowd to Orphelia's pew and introduced the entertainer to Momma and Poppa and then Pearl, who was big-eyed and speechless for once.

"Mr. and Mrs. Bruce, your daughter is blessed to have such an amazing talent," Madame Meritta said. "I would love to include her in my show at the fair. Is there any way we can work something out?"

"Thank you for your offer, but Orphelia cannot participate," Momma said stiffly. "Minstrel music such as what I have heard is not morally uplifting, nor do I approve of proper young Negro women parading themselves before the public singing any songs other than religious."

"Then perhaps you would consider Orphelia singing religious songs during the program, since she is your church's pianist-in-training," Madame Meritta said smoothly. "She could represent your church if you wished, and if Reverend Rutherford is in agreement."

Orphelia looked from Madame Meritta to Momma. Momma's face had gone blank. Orphelia grabbed Poppa's hand and pulled on it. "Can I do it that way?" she pleaded.

"A wonderful idea, Miz Bruce," Miz Rutherford said.

Poppa cleared his throat. He glanced at Momma. "This is something that we'll have to discuss," he said.

"No, we don't, because there is nothing to discuss," Momma said sharply.

"I see," said Madame Meritta. She smiled at Orphelia. "You look so much like your mother. You look familiar, Miz Bruce. Have we met before?"

"Certainly not," said Momma. "Now you must excuse us. It's getting late. We must get home. We don't have coaches to tote us about."

"Madame Meritta, you need to get settled down, too," said Miz Rutherford. She looked so disappointed. "You pull out of here before dawn, don't you? You need your beauty sleep."

Momma spun around and walked away, holding on to Pearl and Poppa by the elbows. Shoulders drooping, Orphelia looked up at Madame Meritta, then at Momma's retreating back. She'd never seen Momma act so rudely to anyone before. She grabbed Madame Meritta's hands. "Thank you for asking, Miz Madame. I really, really prayed that I could have been in your show."

"I understand. But just remember that your time for fame may still come eventually. I would have loved to have you for this World's Fair show. Perhaps there'll be another time."

"Orphelia, Momma said come on!" That was from Pearl behind her. Pearl clasped her hand around Orphelia's elbow and maneuvered her away.

Momma was probably really on fire now. Well, let her be! Madame Meritta had wanted Orphelia in the show! She said Orphelia had amazing talent! That was proof from a famous person's lips. Maybe if Orphelia could just figure out what Momma had against the music she loved, she could still change Momma's mind. She'd missed her chance at next week's show at the World's Fair, but the fair itself didn't end until December. Maybe Madame Meritta would perform there again and would ask Orphelia to join her. And maybe by then Momma would have had a change of heart.

Momma walked like somebody had slid a beanpole down her back. Poppa followed quietly behind.

Pearl pulled at Orphelia's elbow. They had hardly spoken to each other all day. "What'd you think of the Hannibal Twins? I wasn't impressed." She sucked her tooth noisily to show her disapproval. "They do the same song every time. But didn't you just love Madame Meritta's dress! Probably somebody from St. Louis made it just for her. I wish that she had sung something. She *is* prettier than what she looks like on the posters."

Orphelia, however, didn't answer. With a quick look at her, Pearl hurried up to Momma. "I think I'll be a seamstress and make fancy dresses for folks," she said. "Momma, maybe we could go to St. Louis and see the fashions at the fair, and then Orphelia could play and—"

"Be quiet!" Momma snapped. Pearl shut up. Momma turned around and faced Orphelia. "You are *not* going to be in that woman's show ever, and that's final. We are *not* going to the World's Fair because I've heard that we colored will not be treated right there. And St. Louis is much too large and dangerous a city for proper people like us to visit."

"Those are some mighty big pronouncements you just made there, Otisteen," said Poppa. "I wouldn't mind going to St. Louis someday, to tell you the truth. But what I'm most concerned about is you saying that Orphelia—"

"Are we going to argue about this in the road?" Momma folded her arms. "Thelton, the girl is not going to parade herself in a minstrel show."

"But, Momma, Madame Meritta's shows aren't like those—"

"Don't you dare dispute me!"

"Otisteen, listen. You've let this thing build up inside

so till it's ruling you. Orphelia—"

"Be quiet, Thelton." Momma gripped Orphelia by the shoulders. "I said no! And if you keep disputing me, I'll not even allow you to be church pianist-in-training, and you will never play any kind of piano again! So get this foolishness out of your head. I don't care what this Madame Meritta says. I don't care what Miz Rutherford says! And I don't even care what you say, Thelton Bruce!"

Poppa firmly pulled Momma's hands from Orphelia's shoulders. He held Momma's hands in his, but Momma snatched them away. "If you know what's best for you, you'll let me be," Momma said, so low that Orphelia could barely hear her.

Poppa sighed. "The day is apt to come when we'll be sorry we didn't let her follow her dream," he said in an undertone. "Orphelia, there'll be another time, I promise you," he said louder now, "but not this time. Now, everybody, let's go home."

Orphelia stood in the dusty road. Tears rolled down her face. Pearl took her hand and pulled on it. Orphelia followed her sister home.

Later she lay in bed, watching the light from the kerosene lamp flicker on the wall. She wiggled her fingers under the covers, playing the "Lewis County Rag." Momma had never screamed at her like she had tonight. Had she gone crazy?

The last few weeks had been full of Momma's criticisms.

The more Orphelia progressed with her music and her act for the talent show, the angrier Momma had seemed to get with her. Would she really make her stop playing for the church? That would be the cruelest cut of all. If Orphelia couldn't even play for the church, then her life was truly over.

Madame Meritta had said she wanted Orphelia in her show anytime. She had also said Orphelia was blessed with a musical gift. Poppa said that now wasn't the right time. But when *would* the right time be? Never, apparently, if Momma had her way.

Orphelia sat up in bed. Pearl snored softly. Quickly Orphelia packed her schoolbag with an extra pair of underwear and stockings, and the music tablet from the Stone Shed. Slipping on the dress she'd worn to the talent show, she crept out of the house. Orphelia stood on the porch for a moment, listening for sound from inside. She stepped off the porch into the yard. Going to the weeping willow tree, she kicked it, then darted down the road into the darkness.

Orphelia ran until she was far from the house. She slowed down when she realized fully what she was doing. Was this the right thing to do—to run away? Did she know where she was running to? A streak of fear flashed through her. Should she turn around? She could be back inside the house before anybody even knew she'd been gone.

And risk never being able to play piano again.

She quickened her step. When an owl swooped down over her head, Orphelia shrieked and broke into a run.

She reached the Calico Creek school and church grounds. The coaches were still there. Nobody was in sight, and the horses were quiet. *Now is the time and this is the place,* she told herself. But what if she couldn't get in? What if she got caught?

Heart racing, she crept across the yard to the first coach and listened at the door. Snoring came from inside. She tiptoed to the next coach and heard deep breathing there, too.

At the third coach, however, she heard nothing. Slowly and carefully she studied it. She tried opening the door, but it wouldn't budge. She went around to the side, where there was a board covering a window-size opening. She lifted the latch on the board and peered inside, listening. Then, climbing up on the wheel, she dropped her school-bag through the opening and pulled herself in. She tumbled headfirst into the coach and bumped her forehead sharply on something hard. Pain exploded in her head.

Orphelia scrambled over boxes until she was at the back of the coach. Then she listened. Had anyone heard her? When no one came, she curled up on the floor against the wall of the coach, her schoolbag at her side, and cradled her aching head in her hands.

Soon she drifted into a deep sleep.

CHAPTER 4

THE STOWAWAY

A thin shaft of pale light filtering through the cracks of the coach fell upon Orphelia's cheek and woke her up. Shivering as she felt around for her cover, she wondered why Momma hadn't called her and Pearl to get up and help fix breakfast. And why was her head hurting?

Then memory kicked in, and with a surge of panic she sat up. Last night's horror scene of Poppa and Momma shouting in the middle of the road flared up in her mind. Did they both have hysterics? She pressed her fingers against her cheeks, looking around at the collection of greasy barrels and boxes, piles of dirty sacks and rags, the clutter of pans, rolling pins, and dishes. Finally she realized where she was and the bold thing she had done. *I've broke into Madame Meritta's food wagon! I've actually run away to join a traveling minstrel show and become what Momma would label a common gutter girl. Am I crazy?*

Had the coach moved at all, or was she still in the
school yard, where Miz Rutherford and everybody would
find her? How awful and embarrassing that would be—
to have run away to the school yard! Orphelia peered out
through a knothole. Light mist rose from unfamiliar wheat
fields. She also vaguely remembered the swaying of the
coach and the horses' hooves thudding on the dirt road.
I'm not in my old school yard anymore, but exactly where am I?

She touched the big bump on her forehead. At least
the skin wasn't broken.

Talk about trespassing! This was the second time in
two days she'd gone into a place forbidden to her. She was
truly a sinner now.

What would Momma and Poppa and Pearl be saying
at home right now? They had to have realized by this time
that she wasn't there. Had Poppa gone to the sheriff and
rounded up a search party, or had he just walked to the
outhouse and smoked his cigar? Or sat down in his chair
and read the newspaper? Had Pearl become so guilty over
her lies that she finally told the truth? Or was she telling
some bigger ones?

And Momma. *Is she glad her troublesome youngest daughter is gone, or madder at me now because I've run away?* One
thing Orphelia knew for certain: Momma had to be saying, "Ran away! Absolutely not the kind of behavior for
proper young Negro women, according to the standards
of the day!"

The thought made Orphelia smile a little until a mouse ran across her foot. She almost screamed. Then she heard something rattle the coach door. *Hide!* She had just enough time to crawl to a corner behind the door and bury herself under a huge pile of flour sacks and burlap bags. Too late she saw that her schoolbag still lay in full view.

Someone opened the door, shoving it against her. A man, she figured from the heavy footsteps, had stepped in and was moving barrels and boxes around. One fell inches from her head. He yelled something in a strange language right above her. She held her breath. Had he seen her, or her bag?

The door closed. The man was gone. She let out her breath in relief but stayed where she was. In a few minutes she heard a low murmur of voices, and horses whinnying. She smelled coffee and heard the sizzle of salt pork, which made her stomach growl. Finally, after what seemed like an eternity, she heard the jangle of horses' harnesses and felt the coach lurch forward and begin to move. She pulled her schoolbag to her and slipped the strap around her neck. She reached inside and found a carrot left over from yesterday's lunch. Grateful for the food, she munched on it. Soon the coach was swaying again, and she dozed off.

Orphelia woke with a jolt when the coach stopped, but this time no one opened the door. The coach was hot and stinky, and she had to use the outhouse. She could also smell apples and fish and wanted to search the coach for them, but her need for the outhouse was stronger.

Orphelia pushed aside the rags and hid her schoolbag beneath them. She found an overturned metal washtub and stood on it. Looking through the small window where she had entered, she could see outside. The other coaches were gone. Maybe Madame Meritta and her folks had gone into some nearby town for a matinee performance.

She tried to push open the door, but it refused to budge. It was locked from the outside, Orphelia figured. Going back to the window, Orphelia squeezed herself through it and dangled headfirst above the wagon wheel. She grabbed a handlebar that ran alongside the coach, righted herself, and climbed down the wheel to the ground. Straightening her clothes, she looked around and saw no one. She scampered a short distance to a clump of trees and relieved herself.

Orphelia was glad to be out in the fresh air. She wandered back to the storage wagon and walked around to the other side of it. She noticed that its paint was peeling, the lettering had faded, and some of the walls had holes in them. She hoped that Madame Meritta's coaches back in St. Louis were in better condition than this one was. She could see where one whole section had been completely boarded up, except for the spot where the "window" was.

Orphelia mulled over her situation. The World's Fair performance was next Saturday. If Orphelia could remain undetected until they reached St. Louis, Madame Meritta would have to let her stay on. And then Orphelia could also find out where Madame Meritta's maids and butlers and fancy coaches were. And after Orphelia got famous, she'd come back to Calico Creek in furs and feathers and with her own entourage. Wouldn't Momma and Pearl be surprised! Momma would have to be proud of her then.

Wondering what she'd wear during her performance at the World's Fair, and wishing she'd thought to bring along her best dress and shoes, she skipped around the corner of the storage wagon—and froze. A tall man in a tattered gray jacket and black hat stood not two feet from her. He glared at her out of his right eye. His left eye was closed and sunken, the eyelid thick, moist, and wrinkled. He gripped a large bowie knife in his hand. With her heart doing a tap dance in her chest, Orphelia began stepping backward slowly, away from him, until her back struck the coach wall. Trapped!

The man raised his knife. Orphelia flung her arm over her face and tried to scream, but no sound came out. The man reached into his pocket with his other hand, brought out an apple, and cut it in half with his knife. He pushed one half of the apple, including the core, into his mouth and chewed with his mouth open. A line of slobber slid into the black stubble on his chin. Then he sat down on an overturned bucket, chewing and staring at her.

Orphelia took a deep breath and eased a few more feet

from him and the coach. "Hello. Um, is Madame Meritta here?" she asked. The man didn't answer. "Is anybody here? I mean, besides you? Where are we?"

Still not answering, he shoved the other half of the apple into his mouth. A seed stuck to his lower lip. He pulled out a second apple. When he stretched out his neck to swallow, she saw that a thick, ropelike scar ran from one side of his throat to the other. Goose pimples popped out on her arms.

"Well, I guess I'll be going," she said nervously and turned as if to walk away, hoping that he would, too. But the man stayed put. *Now what? I can't climb back in while he's watching!* Her stomach rumbled.

"Little Paradise," the man said, chewing with his mouth open.

"Huh? Oh." It took her a second to realize he was answering her last question. Relieved to recognize the name of the town and glad that he was talking, she relaxed a little. "That apple looks mighty good," she said. "Did you get it from this wagon?"

"Mine!" The man jumped up, knocking over the bucket, waving the knife, and holding the apple high over his head. "Mine, mine, mine!"

"Don't—mister, don't get upset! I—I don't want your apple!" Orphelia held up her hands palm side out to him, hoping to calm him down. But he didn't seem to understand. Instead he whirled around. With great leaping steps

in oversized boots and flapping coat, he bounded through
the wheat fields and on into the woods. He looked like
a human scarecrow.

Orphelia leaned against the wagon in relief, fanning
herself with her hands. Great grumpity gracious, what
a creepy fellow! Momma would have a fit if she knew
her daughter was talking to a strange man, and a hobo
at that! He certainly couldn't have been a member of
Madame Meritta's minstrel show.

At least she knew where she was now. Little Paradise
was a tiny crossroads somewhere south of Hannibal. It
was even smaller than Calico Creek, and it didn't even
have a church or a school. A few Negro families farmed
around here, but she didn't know any of them.

Using the overturned bucket as a stool, Orphelia
climbed back through the window of the storage wagon.
Inside, she stacked up boxes and barrels to make a wall
that she could hide behind. Then she dumped a pile of
flour sacks and burlap bags onto the floor for a bed and
to cover herself with. After she had made her nest, she
found some apples in a bag hanging from the ceiling and
some salted fish, salted pork, and dried beef in barrels
against the wall. She ate a handful of fish and a handful
of beef. Both were good and curbed her hunger, but now
she was thirsty.

Water! She'd have to go back outside. She hadn't seen
a lake or stream nearby, but a source must be close

because the horses had to have it. Once again she climbed out the window. Within reach of the horses were two barrels cut in half lengthwise and full of water. Cautiously she approached the horses, who paid no attention to her. The water looked clean enough. Though she didn't care for horse spit, she'd drunk horse water before, when she and Pearl were in Canton one dry day and were thirsty. She scooped up some water in her cupped hands, sniffed it, then drank.

Once her thirst was quenched, she hoisted herself back into the storage wagon and slipped behind the barrels and boxes. Then she settled herself in among the flour sacks for a long wait.

Her fingers twitched. She pulled the composition book from her schoolbag and studied the music. Was the composer a musician that Madame Meritta might have known? Orphelia would have to show her the book and ask. She lifted her hands to her imaginary piano and began to sing and play.

As she played, Orphelia wondered about the other people who might have lived in Calico Creek long ago. Hardly anybody in Calico Creek had ever said much about Negro history in Lewis County, except to say how happy everybody was when Emancipation came after the Civil War. Everybody who lived in Calico Creek was Negro anyway, except for that white family who had lived in the Stone Shed. She knew when Calico Creek Missionary

Baptist Church and Training School was established, in 1880. She knew about the history of the Stone Shed, or at least part of it. But what about the rest? How did those instruments and that music book get into the Shed?

The horses whinnied outside. Soon Orphelia heard the creaking rumble of wagon wheels and knew the other coaches were returning. *Hide!* She covered herself with flour sacks. Had that evil one-eyed man returned? Would he tell Madame Meritta that she was in their camp? Orphelia heard the sound of the coach door opening.

"You must have been in here straightening up," a man with a foreign accent said. "You made it so neat that I can't find my towels. What a sweet lady! But I prefer them right behind the door. So now you have put them where?"

"I put them nowhere, Othello. Maybe you left them on a clothesline at the last stop." It was Madame Meritta!

Orphelia tried to flatten herself under the bags. Footsteps tapped on the wood floor. "Whew! Smells like rotten fish in here, Othello. Did you leave the lid off the barrel last night?"

She could feel someone—the man?—right above her. She held her breath. "Madame, salted fish smells like that all the time. Have you been moving my barrels, too? Well, here are my towels and my—*Mon Dieu!*" The man jerked Orphelia to her feet, shouting in a language Orphelia didn't know. It sounded like French.

With bags still draped around her head, Orphelia

flailed blindly about. "Let me go!" She snatched off the sacks and came face-to-face with a short, plump, red-faced man with long black hair and a bristly mustache.

"Oh my goodness, girl, what are you doing here?" said Madame Meritta. "Stop, Othello, it's all right," she said. "Well, no, it's not all right, but let her go anyway. What else is going to happen? First the coach breaks down, this tooth is killing me, and now we've got a stowaway!"

Othello released Orphelia. She straightened and smoothed down her dress, her heart pounding so fast she thought it would leap up her throat and out of her mouth. "I'm Orphelia Bruce, from Calico Creek, remember? From last night!"

Nodding and frowning, Madame Meritta placed her palm against her swollen right cheek. "Oh yes, I remember you, but why—how did you get inside my food wagon? Do your folks know where you are? Of course they don't. You've run away! But you can't stay with *us*."

"Well, I won't go back! You said you wanted me to play with you."

"But that didn't mean come with me now, like this! All right, sit down there, be quiet, and listen to me." Madame Meritta motioned for her to sit on the over-turned washtub. "I can't take a girl your age with me. No. Period. And especially not without your people's permission! Don't you understand? Yes, you have talent, but—why, the authorities could say I kidnapped you!"

"But you joined a traveling show when you were twelve," Orphelia said, "and you performed with famous musicians and organized your own—"

"Oh, that's just show-business talk, Orphelia. You can't believe everything you read." Madame Meritta closed her eyes for a moment. "Listen, when freedom came, my mother died. I was a baby having to live from day to day with whoever took me in. I had no choice. I was on the road at that age only because the family that I was living with at the time was on the road, too, but it wasn't show business. A child shouldn't have to be made to work the way I . . . Honey, you have a family! You must go back home!"

"No, and if you send me back, I'll just run off again! Momma said I can't even be a church pianist anymore! I won't be able to play piano at all." Orphelia's heart tumbled as fast as her words rushed out. She grabbed hold of Madame Meritta's skirt.

Othello stood in front of the door with his arms folded, staring at Orphelia like she'd fallen out of the sky. He reminded her of a hairy sausage. "Madame, you must get ready for this evening," he said. "We still must pick up the coach and the others, remember? And your tooth?"

Madame Meritta looked from Orphelia to Othello and back. "How much more complicated can my life get? Orphelia, I can tell that you love music, and that's wonderful. I'm sure your mother will change her mind once you're back home. At any rate, I'm going to have to put you on the train immediately."

"Which means that we'd have to go back to Hannibal, and that's miles away and the last train left there hours ago," Othello said.

"Well then, I'll send her back by horse tonight."

"But not by me!" said Othello.

"Please, please, *please* let me stay at least tonight," Orphelia moaned in the folds of Madame Meritta's skirt. Then she peered up at the woman. "I can clean, I can wash and iron clothes, I can help you get dressed, I can cook—"

"I, and only I, dress the Madame Meritta," Othello said firmly. "And I'm also the cook."

Madame Meritta smiled briefly at Othello. "Othello, you sound so stuffy," she told him. "And *you*, young lady, are quite an actress." She pulled her skirt out of Orphelia's hands. "You are definitely leaving here first thing in the morning. Right now I want you to quit snotting and sit up. Fold these towels, put them back where Othello tells you, and clean up this place. You think it's fun and easy being in a traveling show, but I assure you that it's a lot harder than you can imagine."

"And when I'm done, can I go with you to your show tonight?" Orphelia asked.

"Absolutely not!" Madame Meritta climbed out of the storage coach. "You stay right in this coach until we come back. This tent show is not for children. You'll be safe here. Reuben will keep an eye on you."

"Who's Reuben?" Orphelia asked. Othello pointed. Orphelia looked out the door and saw the creepy, knife-waving, apple-eating, one-eyed man. She let out a groan. Orphelia crumpled up her face at Madame Meritta.

"Reuben, watch her till we get back," Othello shouted, pointing to Orphelia. "Don't let her leave this wagon."

Reuben nodded. He grabbed his overturned bucket chair, plunked it on the ground just outside the door, and sat down. Then he took out a knife—this one was smaller than his other, at least—and began whittling on a piece of wood. He hummed a tuneless song as he carved.

"I'll get you a slop jar for your outhouse breaks. And you can open the door and get fresh air in," said Madame Meritta to Orphelia.

"But, Miz Madame, that man scares me," Orphelia whispered. "Don't make me stay here with him alone!"

Madame Meritta said, "Humph. All the more reason for you to stay inside this wagon, don't you think? You should have thought about scary men with knives before you ran away from your mother. Reuben's a little feeble-minded, but he won't hurt you."

"One of the only people around here we can depend on, as a matter of fact," Othello added. "He does whatever task he's given and never complains."

Madame Meritta pointed a finger at Orphelia. "You'd do best not to concern yourself so much with Reuben as with your own problems. Now come get the broom and mop, and get to work."

Orphelia peeped at Reuben. No matter what Madame Meritta said, it still seemed like his one good eye glittered back at her evilly. She shivered and hurried past.

With Othello's help, Orphelia straightened, dusted, swept, and mopped the inside of the storage wagon. Othello handed her a horse blanket and a few flour sacks. She would sleep in the same corner where she'd been hiding, but only for tonight, he reminded her. He showed her how to latch the door closed from the inside.

"So you wish to be a star like Madame Meritta?" Othello said, stacking his sacks back into neat piles by the door.

Orphelia nodded. "I have a scrapbook of articles about her. There's nobody like her in the whole world, except maybe the Hyers Sisters." She paused from folding the blanket. "Reuben said we were in Little Paradise. Where do we go after here?"

"To Pitchfork Creek for some gala entertaining there. That's our last stop before St. Louis. But as soon as we reach a train stop anywhere, we're putting you on the train."

To change the subject from trains and leaving, Orphelia quickly asked, "What did she mean about show-business talk? And I meant to ask her where her maids and butlers and personal secretary were."

"Maids and butlers? Now that's some *real* exaggera-

tion." He propped one plump boot up on the metal tub
as he rearranged the apple sacks. "You might read anything in a newspaper or on a playbill about us. It's meant
to suck the audience in. Maids and butlers? You obviously
know nothing about real minstrel shows or traveling
troupes. Now, the old minstrel shows where everyone
wore blackface were the shows that made money, gener-
ally because the owner was white. He got the backing
he needed, see? Madame Meritta is an owner, but she's
colored and a woman, and she refuses to black up her
face to satisfy somebody else's idea of what a Negro is
supposed to look like. Many whites still like that kind
of show, and they won't pay to see our show as we are.
Or sometimes the man selling tickets disappears with
the money box, so we lose our cut of the proceeds. Or
someone in our show leaves in a pout, and there we are,
about to open with no pianist or banjo player, or no
Grand Master! So we stay poor."

Orphelia bit her lip as she listened, not sure how to
phrase what she was thinking. "Couldn't *you* pretend to
be the owner? Couldn't she make some money then?"

Othello tapped his forehead. "You see my white skin,
you think, ah, he could pretend to be the owner and then
things would be all right. *Ma chère*—that's French for 'my
dear,' in case you did not know—I am a Creole of color,
from New Orleans. My grandmother was French, and
I could pass for white, but that's not how I choose to live

my life. Plus, Madame Meritta is my wife."

"Oh!" So Madame Meritta and Othello were married. Well, no wonder he was so concerned about her. Orphelia's cheeks burned. He had looked white to her. But she was still confused. "If it's so hard, then why does she keep doing it?"

"Because she has so much music in her heart that she must share it with the world or her heart will explode. She takes her music to the people wherever they may be, no matter what color they are. She has passion, and she performs with passion."

"That's how I feel about music, too. I don't really care about getting money, either," Orphelia said.

"But she does too many shows for pennies, and so many of her audiences are poor people," Othello said. "We have so many bills. We'll never get rich this way."

Orphelia sat down, stunned by Othello's revelations. Maybe Othello meant Madame Meritta didn't make thousands of dollars—just hundreds. Maybe she didn't live in a mansion—instead, maybe a comfortable eight-to ten-room house with only one maid.

Othello held up his hands. "It is getting late. I must prepare Madame for her performance, as well as myself. After we leave, you stay inside this wagon where it's safe. Strange people travel through the countryside at night, and some men are ruffians and not as nice as Reuben."

Orphelia wanted to ask him more about her strange,

one-eyed bodyguard, but Othello was already out the door. Just then Reuben stood up and stretched. He eased around the storage wagon, plopped down in the weeds, and went back to his whittling. Orphelia wondered what he was carving with those big, bony hands of his. They looked too clumsy to carve anything nice. Well, whatever it was, he seemed to be concentrating very hard on it. She closed and latched the door and returned to her spot inside.

To let Othello tell it, Madame Meritta was almost as poor as everybody in Calico Creek! That certainly wasn't how Orphelia imagined a famous singer's life on the road. And if it wasn't true that Madame Meritta lived in luxury, then had she never performed with famous musicians when she was a child? Had she not traveled around the world? Who had lied—the newspapers and playbills, or Madame Meritta? Had she lied about Orphelia's "amazing talent," too?

Worse yet, had running away been a mistake?

Her heart seemed to flip-flop. She pressed her hands against her chest and breathed deeply to calm herself. Maybe disappointment was making her heart carry on so.

After a short while, someone knocked at the door. When Orphelia opened it, she was surprised to find Madame Meritta standing there. She wore a golden gown that sparkled with blue glitter, and a matching blue turban. Part of it hung down over her face to hide her swollen cheek. "We're on our way, but I just wanted to make sure you were all right," she said. "After the show I'm getting this tooth pulled. I can't stand the pain anymore."

"I hope you feel better. And, Miz Madame, I just want to play my music and sing, just like you. I don't care if I never make any money. You'll see!"

But after Madame Meritta left, Orphelia couldn't help thinking again about how difficult Madame Meritta's life must be if she wasn't making much money. How did she pay for her gowns, for the horses' care, for the musicians' food?

And soon Orphelia was going to be put on the train for home, where Momma and everyone would laugh at her, criticize and humiliate her, where her piano playing was doomed. Momma would make her cut down half the willow tree for a switch and beat her every day. Now what was she going to do?

Orphelia's fingers started twitching again. This time, though, instead of playing her imaginary piano, she just sang. She sang "Didn't the Lord Deliver Daniel?" and "Amazing Grace" and "Oh, How I Love Jesus." Feeling better, she stretched and went to the water bucket that Othello had left by the door for her. She took a deep drink. With the tin cup still to her mouth, she unlatched the door to see what, if anything, was happening outside. Reuben stood there. She shrank back.

"You sing good," he said. He had his hat in his hand.

He wiped his mouth with it.

"Oh, thank you," she said, so amazed that he could talk normal that some of the water went up her nose. Leaving the door open, Orphelia pulled up the overturned metal washtub, sat down on it, lifted her fingers in the air, and sang "Swing Low, Sweet Chariot." Reuben had returned to his place on the ground. He nodded his head to the music. She had an audience.

The sun went down and tree frogs sang. Night birds chirped. Bats swooped across the sky. Orphelia felt freer than she had in many days. She wished Madame Meritta were there to hear her. From spirituals, she moved to school songs, then to nursery rhymes that she'd set to her own tunes. Feeling sassy, she tried "Camptown Races."

Then she began singing the bouncy melody to "Lewis County Rag."

Suddenly Reuben jumped up and pressed his hands to his ears. He shouted, "No, no, no, no, no!"

Orphelia flinched and stopped singing. "What's wrong?"

But Reuben didn't answer. He began to moan and mumble something she couldn't make out. Orphelia sprang to her feet. Maybe he was sick. Or maybe he was going to try to hurt her.

"Please," she begged, her voice trembling, "I can't understand what you're trying to say. What's the matter?" But Reuben only moaned, keeping his hands pressed to his ears and rocking from side to side on his feet.

Orphelia began to feel more sorry for him than scared.

"I'm sorry," she said, hoping to comfort him. "What did I do? Whatever it was, I swear I didn't mean it!"

To Orphelia's relief, Reuben gradually began to calm down, but he still didn't say anything.

Orphelia couldn't understand what had happened. This was the second time in two days she had seen an adult get hysterical over her music. Did he not like ragtime?

Well, it didn't look like she was going to get any answers from him. She decided to change the subject. Nodding toward the knife and carving that lay in the grass near him, she asked, "Can I see what you're making with that piece of wood over there?"

"*No!*" Reuben shouted. "They're mine!" He snatched both objects and jumped up, waving the knife in his hand.

Orphelia rushed inside and latched the door. She grabbed up Othello's heavy black skillet and held it over her head.

"You come in here and I'll give you a skillet fit!" she yelled.

Her heart pounded. Finally she lowered the skillet and peeked out the window. Reuben was nowhere to be seen.

Late in the night the coaches returned. Orphelia heard men's voices and that of a woman who was not Madame Meritta. The voices came and went. Orphelia longed to open the door and ask what had happened at the performance, but she thought better of it. She strained to listen through the knothole, unable to make out what was said.

When the voices finally faded away, she unlatched the door and opened it just a crack. Through the crack, she was relieved to see Madame Meritta and Othello sitting on stools by a fire. Madame Meritta was leaning against him, and his arm was around her shoulder. Orphelia went back to her makeshift bed. Seeing them like that made her wonder if Momma and Poppa had made up from their argument. A sudden sweep of sadness rolled over her. Were Momma and Poppa missing her tonight? Would they ever understand how badly she wanted to play the music she loved?

Some time later, she felt the wagon moving. They were on their way to Pitchfork Creek.

CHAPTER 5
PERFORM WITH PASSION!

Orphelia woke up Saturday morning to the clear tones of a woman's contralto voice singing. It reminded Orphelia of bells, or the rich, deep, golden peals of a church organ. In the background, a piano dragged behind the voice. It was Madame Meritta singing, but it wasn't her playing.

When Madame Meritta stopped and started again, the piano was still as poky as molasses. Orphelia giggled. She lifted her fingers into the air, following the song easily. But who in the world was torturing that poor piano? Someone banged on the keys as if hitting them with fists. The noise finally stopped and was quickly replaced by loud, angry voices.

"If I'm playing bad, it's cause that's all you're getting from me till you pay me my money!" a woman shouted.

Orphelia peeked out the window. A woman wearing a blue feather boa around her neck stood in the doorway of the equipment wagon. She was jerking the end of the boa like an angry cat flicking its tail. She jabbed her forefinger at Madame Meritta, who stood on the ground below with her arms folded, face frowned up. "You shorted me five dollars last night, five before that, and five before that," the woman snarled. "Give me my money, Maryanne, else I'm walking, and taking Robert with me!"

"You keep shaking that finger in my face and they're gonna call you 'Nubs,'" Madame Meritta snapped. She glared at the woman like she really would bite that finger off. The feather in her turban poked the air as she bobbed her head back and forth. She blinked her eyes so fast they looked like hummingbird wings. "Lillian, are you threatening to quit? Right before Pitchfork Creek? Knowing I'm down to the bare bones with musicians?"

"I'm tired of you always got to be the star when you said I'd be the featured act. Yes, I'll leave you"—Lillian snapped her fingers—"just like that if you don't give me my money right now."

Madame Meritta snapped her fingers, too. "Then let the screen door hit ya where I'm about to kick ya! And take Robert with you. I can get another Grand Master."

Madame Meritta caught Orphelia's eye. "And you're next!" Orphelia ducked down. *Darn! Too nosy and too slow!*

Orphelia wondered why the woman had called Madame Meritta "Maryanne." She'd heard some of the other musicians call her by that name, too. *"Madame Meritta" must be her stage name,* Orphelia thought as she reached into the beef barrel, pulled out a strip of meat, and bit off a chunk. It was tough as twine, but it was still food. Better get something to eat while she had a chance. The trains she remembered riding on didn't usually have food, and besides, she had no money to buy any with. Momma's fatback and hominy would taste mighty good right now.

Momma. Didn't matter what Madame Meritta said about Momma changing her mind. Momma's brain turned into concrete sometimes. Maybe that's what Pearl knew so well and tried to avoid at all costs, even if it meant lying.

Orphelia had to smile a little. In the day and a half that she'd been gone, Pearl probably had to take over her chores—helping with Friday's washing and ironing, drying the dishes, sweeping and scrubbing all the floors—plus her own work. With all those extra jobs, would Pearl now have to hear Momma's criticisms when she didn't do them perfectly? *Heaven help me if I have to go back today!* thought Orphelia. She'd have to deal with Momma and Pearl both! While Poppa sat in the outhouse smoking. Humph!

"Orphelia!" Othello called out. Was he coming to take her to the train station already? Slowly she opened the door. He held out a tray of hot buttered biscuits and a bowl of something that smelled spicy. "A simple New Orleans specialty for you, *ma chère.*"

"Oh, ain't this nice! Thank you!" Sniffing eagerly, she took the steaming tray and began gobbling down the food.

"This is delicious! I love chicken and rice." Munching on the biscuit, she handed him back the empty bowl and tray, wishing she could have more. She decided that she liked Othello. He seemed to like her, too. "Is this what you call gumbo?"

"This is gumbo, yes," he said, "but with crayfish that I caught from the creek, down the hill there. You call them crawdaddies. Not many folks eat them around here, but we do in New Orleans."

Crawdaddies?! Everybody around Calico Creek only used crawdaddies as bait to catch fish! Ugh! Orphelia broke into a sweat. She clapped her hand over her mouth and waited for her stomach to bring everything back up.

Othello laughed over his shoulder as he left. "Shoo, you won't get sick. Now we need to be off for Pitchfork Creek and get you on a train. Be ready."

When she didn't throw up, Orphelia wiped her face with a flour sack and smoothed back the hair that had loosened from her braids.

She pressed her lips together and took a deep breath. It was now or never.

Orphelia left the wagon through the door. She ran across the yard and up the steps of the equipment wagon. *Perform with passion!* she commanded herself. She sat down at the piano, counted to herself, and began to play and sing "Listen to the Mockingbird" as loudly as she could. Next, even knowing that she risked her chance of getting into heaven by singing sassy songs, she swung into "Camptown Races," "Yankee Doodle Dandy," and "Oh, Dem Golden Slippers."

She saw Madame Meritta and Othello come and stand below her. Without missing a beat, she nodded at them. Some people she didn't recognize joined them, listening. *Show passion!* After one stanza of "Golden Slippers," she popped up from the piano stool and did the cakewalk with an imaginary Cap. *And I'll keep on singing till she makes me stop,* she told herself. When nobody stopped her, she bounced back down onto the piano stool and sang another stanza of "Golden Slippers." She finished with "This Little Light of Mine."

Orphelia stood up, raised her arms to the sky, and then curtsied. Everybody applauded, including Madame Meritta. Only Reuben stood off to the side, motionless, staring at her with that one beady eye of his. A tiny shiver made its way up Orphelia's spine.

She looked away quickly. Madame Meritta was whispering something to Othello. Orphelia bit her lip. *Say you liked it, please!* she begged silently.

Finally Madame Meritta spoke. "Thank you, Orphelia, for that wonderful serenade." Orphelia broke into a grin. "Now come down from the piano so we can pull out and find a train depot."

Orphelia hung her head at the fatal words. Tears blinded her. She stumbled down the stairs.

"That little gal can thump them ivories, Maryanne," said the banjo player, who also took care of the horses. His name was Laphet. "Voice ain't halfway bad, either."

"She can shake a leg, too," said the man Artimus, who played the drums. "And she's a lot prettier than Lillian, tell you that for sure."

"But Artimus, Laphet, she's only twelve years old!" Madame Meritta stamped her foot so hard that Orphelia jumped. "And a runaway. Don't you know what that means? The sheriff'll be on me in a minute for kidnapping!"

"But you don't have a featured act for this afternoon," Othello said. "Unless you mean *Bertha*." He drew out the woman's name, glancing up at the sky like he was horrified at the thought.

"If *Bertha* even shows up," said Artimus, a slender, brown-skinned man whose booming voice reminded Orphelia of Reverend Rutherford's. "She's so sometimey; tell you one thing, do another. She's liable to be still hangin' out in St. Louie, singin' and dancin'."

Madame Meritta continued to argue with Othello, Artimus, and Laphet. Orphelia thought of something else. "Madame Meritta, ma'am," she broke in as politely as she could. "I have a newspaper article with a picture of you singing with the Magnificent Missouri Colored Minstrels. You were maybe thirteen or fourteen, but you wore a baby bonnet and a baby gown and you had a rattle in your hand. The paper said all minstrel shows had a person who played that character. Can't I play that in your show, too?"

Madame Meritta's hazel eyes got so dark they looked black. "You obviously are too ignorant to know that that 'character' is an insult to our race. It's meant to degrade and poke fun at black children. When I was old enough not to have to perform in that capacity, I stopped. No one—absolutely no one—in my shows has ever performed as one of those, and you won't, either. Orphelia, please understand that your talent isn't the issue. Show business is the issue. This life isn't for a child. You'll have no play-mates, no schooling, no free time, no—"

"I don't mean to sound sassy, but I hear that your shows aren't making much money right now. Without me, you won't have a featured act, like what Mr. Othello just said, and then you'll make even less because the people'll want their money back, won't they?"

Madame Meritta jerked her head back like Orphelia had slapped her. "Who told you that?"

Orphelia pointed at Othello, who nodded. Madame Meritta threw Othello a frown that gave her pretty face more wrinkles than a raisin.

"Madame, we need this girl," Othello said in a soothing voice. "Just for this afternoon. If no one says anything to the sheriff about her, then no one will know. She'll be much easier to work with than that old hateful Lillian. Better piano player, too. I'll never know what you saw in that woman. Madame, we—let's take a walk."

They went behind the equipment wagon. Orphelia stood nearby, watching their lips move as they whispered and shook fingers at each other. Artimus, Laphet, and the other musicians went back to packing their gear.

When she peeked at them again, Othello was smiling. Madame Meritta gave out a long, loud "Oh, *all right, Othello!*"

Was that a good sign? When Madame Meritta called her name, Orphelia hurried over. She wiped her sweaty face with her hands and tried to think of what to say next in her favor if the news was not good.

"All right, you can perform—just this one time," Madame Meritta said.

"Oh, thank you!" Orphelia wrapped her arms around the woman's waist, which smelled like lavender and talcum powder. "Thank you, thank you, thank you!"

"As soon as we find an office, we're sending a telegram to your family, and first thing tomorrow morning, you're getting on that train. You understand?"

"You won't be sorry. I'll be so good! I'll—"

"You'll hold your tongue is what you'll do," Madame Meritta said sternly. She tilted Orphelia's face up with her finger and gazed deeply into her eyes. "Don't you ever tell anybody that my shows don't make money, you hear? This is serious business, and you know nothing about my kind of audiences, no matter what your sassy little tongue says."

"Yes, ma'am," Orphelia said. She hugged Madame Meritta again. Her chance—her chance at last!

"It's a mystery how you can win over Othello and me but you can't get your mother to accept your music, eh?" Madame Meritta teasingly pinched her on the cheek.

Orphelia stared back at her somberly. "Momma doesn't understand that I just got to play my piano and sing, no matter what. It's like the songs gotta come twisting out of my heart. You know what I mean?"

"More than you could ever know."

Othello approached, shaking his head and looking distressed. Orphelia had a horrifying thought. Had he changed his mind about her? Could he make Madame change her mind again, too?

"I can't find Lillian's outfit." He was so frowned up, his mustache was really bristling now. "I bet she and Robert took their costumes with them, which weren't theirs to take. Bless their thieving hides!"

Madame Meritta explained to Orphelia that Lillian had played an orphan boy and wore a coat, trousers, derby, blouse, stockings, and brogans. "Now where are we going to find clothes like that to fit you by this afternoon?"

One bad thing after another! Orphelia thought. She kept quiet. Would lack of the right clothes keep her from her biggest chance?

"Time to go. Maybe we can find something in my trunks." Madame took Orphelia by the hand and headed for her sleeper coach. "Othello, Artimus, everybody, on to Pitchfork Creek!"

Orphelia followed the woman to the coach, where Artimus sat waiting in the wagon seat with the horses' reins in his hands. He was also the stage manager and the repairman. Orphelia struggled to keep a dignified appearance, but it was hard to keep from leaping and screaming with joy. *One step at a time,* she told herself. *If I'm good enough this afternoon, maybe she won't put me on that train.* "Did you like my songs? What time do I come on? How long do I sing? Can I dance, too?"

"You can hush up until I can sit down and think," Madame Meritta said. Orphelia climbed up after her into the sleeper coach and froze. *This* was where Madame lived when she was on the road?

Lined up against one wall inside the coach were three beds as thin as stretchers. Humpback trunks and stacks of boxes bulging with papers, shoes, and other items spilled over by each bed. A tattered brown and yellow carpet covered part of the rough wood floor. At one end of the coach sat a monstrous dresser with a basin and cracked pitcher, and jumbled trays of toiletries. Opposite the beds was a full-length mirror with pictures, posters, and postcards plastered around the edges. Three large, doorless cabinets were crammed with gowns, coats, and scarves. Other garments swayed on hooks suspended from the ceiling in the remaining corners and crevices of the coach. A thick, stale fragrance of lavender, talcum, pomade, and camphor choked the hot air. Slop jars were probably under the beds, too. Orphelia hoped Madame Meritta wouldn't give *her* the job of emptying them.

Madame sat down on one of the beds and removed a pile of clothes from the top of a trunk. "Pull that green curtain open so we can get some fresh air. And sit down."

Orphelia squeezed past a hook of clothes and sat down by Madame Meritta. "How many people live in here?" The whole coach didn't seem to be much bigger than her and Pearl's room back home. Trying to keep from frowning, she slapped at a fly.

"Counting Lillian, me, and Bertha—the one in St. Louis—usually three women. Sometimes four or five when we're really busy. It can get crowded in here, but I can't afford a private coach for me and Othello. You can take Lillian's bed there if you need to rest on the way."

Madame Meritta banged on the wall, and the coach began to move.

Your railroad coaches and private dining cars are in St. Louis, huh? Orphelia wanted to ask, but she didn't.

As if Madame Meritta had read her mind, she said, "I do travel by rail from time to time. I have a lot more room in boxcars, but trains are expensive. I've had to patch together the coaches we're using right now. This is a hard life, Orphelia."

"Well, I've been meaning to ask how come you don't

have a Mr. Interlocutor. Why's your main man called a Grand Master instead?"

"A Grand Master is almost the same thing, but he doesn't have to play the straight man and be the butt of the other actors' jokes. I want my master of ceremonies to be taken seriously, not made out to be some kind of fool. I don't have a Mr. Bones and Mr. Tambo, either. They're the 'end men' in minstrel shows—you know, the comedians who poke fun at Mr. Interlocutor. And I don't have female impersonators or jugglers, the way most minstrel shows do. In fact, Orphelia, I don't really have a true minstrel show. I'm a musician, and I want pure music and dance. My core group is pretty much with me now, except for some folks still in St. Louis.

"It seems like minstrel shows are evolving anyway," Madame Meritta continued. "There's vaudeville and music theater. New people are coming in and forming all kinds of shows that they don't even call 'minstrel' anymore. But it's exciting, too, Orphelia. I met a girl down in the heel of Missouri singing a sad, sad song in a tent show, but with that old Missouri stomp beat. A woman I was sitting by said that kind of music was going to be as big as ragtime in a few years. She said that now they're calling it 'the blues,' and colored women blues singers are gonna hit it big. You don't see many colored women playing ragtime, but this blues—it just makes you pull your heart out your mouth and show it to everybody."

"I've never heard of blues music. I think I've felt that way a lot, though," said Orphelia.

"If I had my dream come true, I'd buy a building in St. Louis, turn it into an opera house, and bring in all those first-class music shows like Black Patti's Troubadours and the Fisk Jubilee Singers."

"I've heard of them!" Orphelia said. She leaned forward, eager to know more about Madame Meritta's plans. "What else would you do?"

Madame Meritta began to dig around in a trunk. "I wouldn't be out on the road like this, that's for sure. I've been out here since I was twelve, and I'm tired."

"But don't you want to still travel around the world?" This person sitting by Orphelia was sounding less and less like the fabulous Madame Meritta, star of the Traveling Troubadours, and more and more like an ordinary woman. Orphelia hunched over, put her chin on her hand, and looked out the window at the fields of wheat and corn passing by.

"People change, my dear." Madame Meritta paused in her searching. "I want to settle down and give music lessons to aspiring singers."

"Like me?" Orphelia sat up straighter. Madame Meritta shrugged and went back to digging without answering.

Orphelia knelt beside her and peered into the trunk. She pulled out a gray uniform coat with brass buttons. It reminded her a little of the one Uncle Winston had on in his portrait. She had to fight off a wave of homesickness. "My uncle, my momma's brother, played a cornet. He's dead now, though." She sighed. "Do you think maybe I could wear this in the show?"

"Oh, chile, no, that's way too big for you. It used to be one of Robert's costumes — I guess that thieving scoundrel didn't make off with everything after all. Maybe I'll give it to Reuben. He has one like it, but it's pretty old and tattered."

At the mention of Reuben's name, Orphelia shuddered, suddenly recalling his crazy outburst the night before and the look on his face this afternoon. Should she tell Madame Meritta about it? Yesterday Othello had been singing Reuben's praises. Would Madame Meritta get mad at Orphelia now, accuse her of upsetting him? But what if Reuben really was dangerous?

"That Reuben is pretty strange," she began. "Last night while you all were gone, I was singing in the wagon. He got real upset all of a sudden."

"Upset how?" Madame Meritta stopped rummaging through the trunk but didn't look up.

Orphelia told her what had happened. Then she waited to be scolded.

But Madame Meritta only said, "Yes, he does act in odd ways sometimes."

"How did he end up here with you all?" asked Orphelia.

Madame Meritta explained that they'd found Reuben

some years ago. They were returning from Keokuk, Iowa, and were coming through northeast Missouri. They were camped near the Mississippi River not far from Hannibal.

Madame held up a shirt, shook her head, and held up another. "Way late that night I was doing something— I forget what—at the edge of the camp. And I felt this wet, slimy hand on my shoulder. I screamed! Othello and everybody came running. Here was this man, so dirty and raggedy and skinny he looked like he'd crawled out of a grave in the backwaters. The man collapsed as soon as Othello grabbed him. We fed him and cleaned him up. He could barely talk. Had scars and scabs all over him. When we left to go on to St. Louis, he followed us—on foot—for so many miles that Othello took pity on him. He's been with us ever since."

Orphelia shivered, remembering the long, ropelike scar that stretched from one side of his neck to the other. "He was doing all right till I was singing the melody to 'Lewis County Rag.' Then he got the hysterics."

"He has some sort of mental problem," Madame explained. "After we took him in, we tried to find out where he was from and what had happened to him that put him in such a terrible state, but he never could tell us. We just made up the name Reuben for him."

Orphelia sat back on her heels. How kind and generous Madame Meritta and Mr. Othello were for taking Reuben in. They didn't seem to mind his odd behavior or his hideous appearance or his mysterious past. As far as Othello was concerned, Reuben was hardworking and loyal. Orphelia began to feel a little ashamed for being so suspicious of him. Maybe he really wasn't a bad man after all. Still, Orphelia couldn't help feeling uneasy about him.

Madame Meritta took out a package wrapped in white linen and pulled out a boy's blue jacket, white silk shirt, cummerbund, trousers, and derby. "Oh, dear," she said softly. Then, to Orphelia's amazement, Madame Meritta's face crumpled up. She pressed the jacket to her heart.

Orphelia reached out and touched her on the arm. "What's wrong?"

"Nothing." Madame Meritta sniffed a couple of times, straightened, then briskly shook the coat in the air. "See if you can make these fit. They're not doing anybody any good molding away in this trunk."

Orphelia examined the jacket, richly embroidered in white at the cuffs and collar, on both panels, and on the back. "It's beautiful. Whose is it?"

"Well, if you must know, it belonged to my son, Ralston. He would have been fifteen years old this year." Madame Meritta fell silent.

Orphelia was stunned. "What happened to him?" she asked.

"He died of smallpox two years ago. He's buried in a small cemetery in New Orleans. He went everywhere with me, but he never performed. And then that August we were in New Orleans. He fell ill, and there was nothing I could do to save him. I've always felt that had I not been on the road, he never would have gotten sick, and he'd still be with me now."

Orphelia peered up at Madame Meritta. The older woman's eyes were large and wet. "Othello never got over it, either." She glanced down at Orphelia. "Well, come on, Orphelia, try it on," she said, all business again. "We've still got to get your act together."

Orphelia saw Madame Meritta's eyes glisten as she turned away. Quickly Orphelia removed her dress and drew on the clothes. Everything was too big, but before Madame Meritta could tell her to remove them, Orphelia rolled up the shirt and pant cuffs and pushed back the jacket sleeves.

"Look, Miz Madame. This will work all right, won't it? Please say it will!"

Orphelia couldn't tell if Madame Meritta was gazing at her or just at the clothes. How would Momma react if she knew her daughter was wearing boys' clothes! And Pearl would have to talk about the old-fashioned cut of the jacket, but she would love the needlework. After what seemed like forever, Madame Meritta spoke. "All right. It's just this one time, anyway."

CHAPTER 6
A CLOSE CALL

O rphelia's heart pounded. "The
Grand Extraordinaire"—which
was what Madame Meritta's Pitchfork
Creek gala was entitled—was under
way. Orphelia stood at the back of
the tent. She swallowed nervously and
adjusted the derby on her head again.
She pulled at the cummerbund, the
wide belt around her waist.

In a few minutes Othello, who would serve as Grand
Master in place of Robert, would give her the signal.
Then she was to run down the center aisle to the stage,
hurry up the steps to the piano, and sing "Ballad of a
Homeless Child."

She wiped her face with the back of her hand and
tried to calm herself. The tent was the biggest she'd ever
seen or been in—bigger even than the one at Hannibal's
Emancipation Proclamation program. And the people!
It seemed like a thousand folks, mostly Negro but many

whites, too, had crammed into the tent. She bet they came from as far away as Clarksville, Little Paradise, and maybe even St. Louis! Her heart was beating faster than it ever had.

This would be Orphelia's first and last chance to perform before a real audience. They had passed a tiny train station on their way into Pitchfork Creek. True to his word, Othello had dropped Reuben off there to give a message to the telegraph man for Orphelia's parents. The note said that first thing in the morning, she would be carted back by train to Canton, where her parents were supposed to pick her up. The note also requested that they pay for the ticket.

By this time tomorrow she would probably be back in Calico Creek. For the rest of her life, she would be forced to play only on her pretend piano. Momma would rope her to the washtub, where she would wash clothes forever and die an old maid. Pearl would marry Cap, have ten children, and continue to tell lies, and Poppa would just smoke himself to death in the outhouse. She tried not to be mad at Poppa, but she was, a little.

Was doing this performance a mistake? *What if I trip on these pants and fall flat on my face in front of everybody? What if I forget the words to the song? What if—*

There! The signal! Othello had just swept his arms high into the air. The band struck up the opening bars of "Homeless Child." Orphelia gulped and froze.

He raised his arms again, but she still couldn't move. *Have I had a heart attack and died standing on my feet?*

Othello stepped closer to the edge of the stage. The music faded. "Ladies and gentlemen . . . Orville, our Musical Orphan Boy Prodigy, will capture your hearts with a most sorrowful, heart-wrenching song. Please prepare yourselves with handkerchiefs. Orville, my child, please come forward to the stage now! *Please come forward now!*"

At the sound of his voice, Orphelia came out of her trance. *Perform with passion,* she told herself. She doubled up her fists and rushed through the aisle between the rows of red and brown and yellow and black and white faces and gaping mouths, up the steps and to the piano. The band, which had swung into the chorus of "Homeless Child," played softer now, waiting.

As soon as Orphelia's fingers touched the piano keys, she relaxed. She began singing the first mournful stanza. Gaining confidence, she moved into the chorus and quickened the beat, tapping her foot and bobbing her head. She looked out at the crowd. The people were nodding, and some began clapping in time to the faster beat. They liked it!

When she came to the last stanza, she stood up and sang, "With a loving mother, I'll never be homeless again." She strutted around at the edge of the stage, then faced the audience with her hands poised on her hips, singing. The audience was right there with her, standing, smiling, and applauding. A woman near the back of the tent waved her green and white handkerchief in time to the music.

They like me! They like me! Miz Madame will have to let me stay now.

At the end of the song, Orphelia threw her hands up in the air and struck a pose. Remembering the boy who had portrayed Abe Lincoln in the talent show, she folded her arm across her waist and bowed deeply, like he did. But her hat fell off—just like his had—revealing her braided hair. The derby rolled to the end of the platform, dropped off, and wobbled down the center aisle.

Aghast, Orphelia looked helplessly over to Othello, who shrugged, smiled, and applauded. The audience broke into laughter.

A man in the front row rescued her hat. He walked up to the stage and, with a big smile, handed the derby back to her. Orphelia took the hat. "Thank you," she said. Glancing again at Othello, she bowed to the man. The audience broke into an even louder round of applause.

I bet they think he's part of my act. Smiling gloriously, her sweaty face shining with victory, she bowed to him again.

Othello came out onto the stage and took her hand. "Orville, the Musical Orphan Boy Prodigy. Or should I say *Miss* Orville, the Musical Orphan *Girl* Prodigy? Isn't she wonderful?"

As the audience applauded, a group of men who had been standing at the back of the tent now headed toward the front, talking and laughing loudly. Pushing and shoving one another, the men found seats. Then one of them pointed to Orphelia and Othello and yelled, "Hey, put some black on that gal! Better go get you some cork and put some black on you, too, fat boy!"

The other men stamped their feet and began to shout, "Black 'em up, black 'em up, black 'em up!" They were joined in the chant by some of the white members of the audience who suddenly didn't seem as friendly as before. Some Negro members of the audience stood up and began to leave, looking over their shoulders nervously.

"Get off the stage," Othello said in a low voice to Orphelia. "Hurry!" Orphelia left the stage and ran to the musicians' pit, where Laphet stood, holding his banjo like a bat. "What's the matter? Did I do something wrong?" she asked.

Out of nowhere Reuben appeared, scooping her up in his arms. "Get away, get away, Otisteen!" he hissed, with a terrible expression on his face.

Otisteen?! Did he just— She screamed and struggled to break free, but he held on tightly to her. "Wait! What did you say? That's my Momma's—how did you—ow! Put me down! What's going on?"

"No time! No time! Get away, Otisteen!" Reuben swept her out of the tent.

Madame Meritta saw them and came running. "Thank the Lord. Oh, thank you, Reuben." Reuben set Orphelia on the ground, and Madame Meritta grabbed her hand. "Honey, are you okay? Reuben, go find Othello and see if he needs help rounding up the others." Reuben darted off.

Orphelia could hear Othello shouting above the noise, "Please, let us have calm! Everything is all right!"

To a tall, plump woman dressed in a stunning blue gown and lace bonnet and twirling a matching parasol, Madame Meritta said, "Bertha, you may have to drive this time. Take *her* with you."

Without a word, Bertha pushed back her bonnet, lifted the skirt of her gown with one hand, and grabbed Orphelia's hand in her other. Dragging Orphelia with her, she ran across the yard to the equipment coach and pushed Orphelia through the door. Then she climbed up on the wagon seat and picked up the horses' reins. Orphelia scrambled to the window and peeked out. What was going on? What had she done? And why on earth had Reuben just called her Otisteen?

She saw Othello, Madame Meritta, and the other band members stride from the tent, surrounded by a ring of white men with their guns drawn. "Oh, are they gonna shoot?" Orphelia cried.

"Those are the sheriff's men," Bertha shouted back, "so I hope not." When Artimus scrambled up into the wagon seat by Bertha and took the reins, she hurriedly climbed down and pushed into the coach with Orphelia.

The sheriff's men formed a protective circle around

the wagon to fend off the growing crowd of white men, who were shouting threats and cursing. "We want our money back!" somebody yelled. Madame Meritta, Othello, and Laphet pushed through the crowd and squeezed into the wagon while the rest of the troupe members made their escape to other coaches. Orphelia didn't see Reuben anywhere. She hoped he was all right. He did save her, after all, and she was grateful. And she also needed to ask him how he knew her mother's name.

Frightened by the noise, one of the horses reared. With the coach tilting dangerously, Artimus snapped the reins and drove off.

Everyone inside the coach was silent as it lurched over the rough road leading them out of Pitchfork Creek. Shoved up between Bertha and Laphet in her hot jacket and trousers, Orphelia could barely breathe. She tried to get some meaning of what exactly had happened by peeking at the faces of the men and women around her, but their expressions didn't tell her anything.

Madame Meritta's head was turned toward the coach window, which had been closed for safety. Othello kept stroking his mustache, as if making sure it was still there.

Orphelia remembered how the men had shouted at her and Othello to "black 'em up, black 'em up," but in all the commotion, she hadn't understood. Now she did. They wanted her and Othello to put that burnt cork on their faces, and the men had a hissy fit when Othello refused. It was so brave of him to face that mob!

Still, if she hadn't wasted so much time by taking so many bows and dropping her derby, she would have been off the stage by the time the men reached the front. The dancers would have come on, and maybe the men wouldn't have thought about her not being in blackface.

"Guess we're having shoe soup tonight," Laphet said.

"Yep. I was counting on making a little piece of change myself, but ol' trouble came along and took it away," said Bertha.

Orphelia tried to follow their conversation, but it made no sense other than that she was sure they were talking about what had happened. "Each of you will be paid your dues," Madame Meritta said, "even if I have to sell all my coaches."

"Oh, I'm not complaining," said Bertha quickly. "This isn't the first time some devil disrupted a show and kicked my money down the drain, and it won't be the last."

Everybody talked at once, saying how things were a shame and that Pitchfork Creek deserved its name because so many devils lived there. "And to holler and shout and threaten a little girl the way they did," Laphet added, looking at Orphelia.

"It was my fault, wasn't it, for taking so much time getting off the stage," Orphelia whispered miserably.

"Oh no, no, no, not you!" Laphet and Madame Meritta said together.

Othello tapped Orphelia on the knee. "Those ruffians just wanted to start a fight. They knew if they could get something started, the sheriff would close us down. I wouldn't doubt but that another show hired them to do just that so they could come and take our place. The sheriff was good to protect us."

Madame Meritta turned her head, and Orphelia could see that her eyes were puffy. "We'll play Pitchfork Creek again. We've played it before with no problems."

Orphelia sat back against the coach wall, trying not to cry herself. Somehow it still felt like it was her fault. Everything had seemed to be going so well during her act. People had been enjoying her music. Madame Meritta was right. Life on the road wasn't at all like she thought it would be. Maybe Momma really did know what she was talking about when she said show business was not where proper young Negro women—or at least Orphelia— needed to be. It was *dangerous!*

Yet she still felt the flood of excitement she had experienced standing on that stage singing and playing the piano, with the people applauding her. Her first "professional" appearance only made her hungry for more.

The equipment wagon finally rolled into a clearing, followed by the other coaches. Everyone climbed out and began jabbering all at once. Orphelia was relieved to see that Reuben was with them. She left the coach and took off her jacket, glad to be in the open air again at last. But even with the jacket off, she still felt a heavy weight pressing down on her shoulders. Knowing she would have to go back home in the morning filled her with dread.

"I grabbed her," Reuben said. "Othello, did you see me? I saved her."

"Yes, Reuben," Othello said with a smile, "you did a good job."

Orphelia looked up at him humbly. "Thank you, Reuben."

He smiled proudly.

"But why did you call me Otisteen?" she added.

Reuben's face clouded over. Orphelia waited for him to say something, but he just stood there, looking confused.

"What are you talking about?" Madame Meritta asked.

"Before," Orphelia explained, "when Reuben was carrying me out of the tent, he called me Otisteen. That's my momma's name. How do you know my momma's name, Reuben?"

He shrugged and turned away momentarily.

"Orphelia, I'm sure that's not possible," said Madame Meritta. "What with all the noise and confusion, you probably just heard him wrong. I'm surprised you were able to hear anything above that din!"

"I guess you could be right," Orphelia said. But she wasn't really convinced.

Finally Reuben spoke. He muttered sadly, "Bad luck,"

and his face pulled into a deep frown.

"Well, they say it *can* be bad luck to have a child along," broke in Bertha, looking at Orphelia like she was a voodoo doll.

"No, no, don't say that, Bertha," Othello said.

"Well, all I'm saying is how Maryanne got that terrible toothache, Lillian and Robert quit, and now this — in just a few days' time."

So now Orphelia was bad luck? Was that why Madame Meritta didn't encourage musicians to bring their children with them? Orphelia backed away from Bertha and Reuben. "I guess it's good, then, that you're putting me on that train, huh?" she said. She felt lower than a snail's belly.

"The train!" Madame Meritta groaned. She cradled her face in her hands. "Oh, I forgot about the train! But we can't stay here overnight now. It's not safe! Who knows what those troublemakers might be up to? Oh, Lord, do preserve my sanity."

"Madame, I think you are right," Othello said. He pointed at the western sky, where dark clouds stretched like a greenish-black blanket. "And that rain we left behind Thursday night is about to catch up with us. It could be pretty bad. I believe it's best we move on. We will have to try to catch the train at another stop."

"I think we better keep going too," said Laphet.

Madame agreed. She ordered the camp to break up. After the coaches had been secured, Orphelia climbed into the sleeper coach with Madame Meritta and Bertha. With the sleeper coach in the lead, the caravan pulled off.

Orphelia lay back wearily on her bed, thinking about the events of the day. Of everything that had happened, the thing that still troubled her the most was Reuben calling her Otisteen. She was sure she had heard him correctly. But maybe it was just a coincidence—maybe he knew someone else by that name. After all, there was no way he could have known who Orphelia's momma was. Orphelia was sure she had not seen him around the night of the talent show in Calico Creek.

Unless Reuben had been in Calico Creek some other time. The thought made Orphelia uncomfortable. No one knew anything about Reuben's past. Maybe he had been a hobo, like Cap—or worse yet, some sort of ruffian running from the law. Cap said that the Stone Shed was a popular stop for transients. Maybe Reuben had hidden out there.

The Stone Shed was also where Orphelia had discovered the music for "Lewis County Rag"—the song that had sent him into fits. Could there be a connection? Maybe he had heard the song played when he was there. But why would it bother him to hear the song again?

The only thing Orphelia knew for sure was that some strange things were beginning to trouble her about Reuben.

Later Orphelia lay on Lillian's old bed with her schoolbag for a pillow. "Thanks for giving me my chance, Miz Madame," she said.

"You were marvelous." Madame paused from writing in her ledger. "You're a curious young lady. You really are determined, aren't you? You remind me of myself a little, when I finally got bit by the show-business bug."

"I do?" Orphelia beamed proudly.

"Honey, you moved that audience so much with your singing that they turned the place into a riot!" Bertha burst out laughing. "Now if that ain't some kind of genius, I don't know what is!" Bertha fell back against the bed, she was laughing so hard. Madame Meritta laughed, too.

Orphelia crossed her arms and pursed her lips. That didn't sound funny to her. "Why're you laughing at me? What's so funny?"

"Baby, we're just playin' with you," said Bertha. She struggled up to a sitting position, still chuckling. "You come onstage with your little ol' self and sing, and people go crazy. You got star quality. Keep hold to it."

"It's good to laugh, Orphelia," Madame Meritta said gently. "After all we've been through these past two days, it's good to laugh instead of cry. By the time you *do* get back home, you'll be a real trouper, just like us."

Orphelia thought about the day's exciting activities. She saw herself onstage over and over as "Orville, the Musical Orphan Boy Prodigy," with the people cheering and waving at her. And then she saw herself in a stunning gown like Madame Meritta's, surrounded by adoring fans. Madame Orphelia, musical star! She drifted off to sleep.

Sometime later, in the middle of the night, she was awakened by sharp, earsplitting booms. Gunshots? She sat up straight. Were the men in those tents after them again? When the sky lit up, she realized the sounds were claps of thunder, and she was seeing lightning. Soon the coach was being pelted by hail and heavy rain. The coach swayed as the storm bore down on them.

Orphelia curled up around her schoolbag with her hands over her ears. Poppa had always said that thunder could never hurt her, but it still frightened her. A few minutes later, she felt rain drip down on her head from a rent in the coach roof. She scrambled to another spot, but soon the roof was leaking there, too. Orphelia pulled a thin blanket over her head. She could feel the coach moving slower and lurching as the horses strained to pull their load through the muddy road.

Finally the coach stopped. Peeking out from under the blanket, Orphelia saw Madame Meritta pounding on the wall. "Othello, are you all right?" she said. "Why are we stopping?"

"I am fine," Orphelia heard him holler back through the rain. "The bridge, however, isn't in as good shape. I can see the stream from here, and it's over its banks. I can't see the bridge, so I assume that it's been washed away.

We'll camp here till morning and see what damage has been done."

Orphelia pulled the blanket back over her head and shifted her body to another dry spot on the bed. Now the bridge was out. She felt a tiny streak of satisfaction. If the bridge was out, maybe the train track was out, too.

CHAPTER 7

THE DIXIE PALACE

Orphelia stood under a brilliantly
blue spring sky Sunday morning
with Madame Meritta, Othello, and the
other musicians, listening to Laphet
read from the Bible. Earlier that morning, when she had looked outside, she
discovered that Othello was right—the
bridge was gone. All that was left were
a few black pilings sticking up on the bank by a
roiling, writhing, debris-filled brown river. It continued
to suck off chunks of earth from the bank as it stormed
over its old creek bed.

"May the Lord watch between me and thee, while
we are absent, one from another. Let us all say amen,"
prayed Laphet. He also served as a deacon at his church
in St. Louis. Orphelia joined in with the others in saying
amen. Back at Calico Creek Missionary Baptist Church,
the congregation was probably saying the same words.
A wave of homesickness hit her. If she were there, she'd

be at the piano. Or would Momma have intervened already and forbidden her to play this morning?

"What else are we going to do today?" she asked Madame Meritta when the service ended. Orphelia was hoping to have some time on her own. She'd decided it was time to find out more about Reuben, and there was only one way to do that—she'd have to spy. He wasn't going to be able to give her any answers himself, she knew by now.

"Today we rest," Madame Meritta replied, "because we don't work on Sunday. This is the Lord's day. Probably some of the fellas will scout around to see what the stream looks like further down or see if there's another bridge. I just wish there was some way to get a message to your folks—they'll be frantic when you don't get off that train in Canton today."

Orphelia went back to the sleeper coach. She took off her muddy shoes and smelly stockings and lay down on her bed. Though it was stuffy inside, it was still cooler than being outside in the midday sun.

Fate had given her a few more hours to live with the minstrel show. With the bridge out, it would take longer for them to reach the next train stop. But on the other hand, until the bridge could be replaced or the water went down or they found another route, they couldn't reach St. Louis, either.

Orphelia reached into her schoolbag and pulled out

the composition book she'd taken from the Stone Shed.
She still hadn't had a chance to examine it closely, and
now she thought again about Reuben's puzzling reaction
to "Lewis County Rag." She opened to that page and
studied the notes carefully, as if they might give her some
clues.

Orphelia continued to thumb through the pages of
the notebook. Tucked behind the last page was a folded-up
piece of newsprint. She unfolded it carefully and saw that
it was the front page of the Hannibal newspaper, dated
August 8, 1892.

She scanned the stories. A tornado touched down on
the southern outskirts of Canton last week . . . a steamboat sank in the Mississippi . . . wholesale prices of hogs
remained steady. . . . Then a headline caught her eye—
"Riot at Dixie Palace Ends in Assault Charges Against
Two Negroes."

She started to read.

*What began as a musical tribute to the Mississippi
River heritage in Lewis County on August 1 ended in
a melee with at least one injury. The scene of the disrup-
tion was the famous Dixie Palace, a popular facility in
Calico Creek where young and old regularly gather on
Saturday afternoons to partake in social pleasantries.*

*On this date, a Negro musical group called the Bruce
Trio, which consists of Thelton Bruce, his wife Otisteen,*

*and her brother Winston Taylor, all of Calico Creek,
were engaged in singing and performing on their instruments for the attendees.*

Stunned, Orphelia stopped and reread the words.
Momma, Poppa, and Uncle Winston playing music? Where
in the world was the Dixie Palace? This was something
they had never told her.

She read on.

*Witnesses say that Taylor became abusive with a
white citizen and assaulted him. A group of men came
to the citizen's rescue and held the three Negroes, and the
sheriff's deputies were called. The woman was released,
but Taylor and Bruce were taken to the county jail.
Taylor was charged with assault with intent to commit
bodily harm.*

*Enraged that a white citizen had suffered injuries at
the hands of a Negro, friends of the victim approached
the jail to teach Taylor a lesson. They entered the jail,
removed Taylor, beat him, and dumped him into the
Mississippi for good measure. Satisfied that justice had
been done, the sheriff dismissed charges against Bruce,
and the Dixie Palace was shut down until further notice.
Sheriff's officials say that although Taylor's body has not
been found, he is presumed to be dead.*

The story continued on the other side of the page. Orphelia turned it over. A large picture of the Bruce Trio stared back at her. Momma, Poppa, and Uncle Winston. She realized with a shock that it was the same picture that she'd seen on the handbill back home. And there was also a photograph of the Dixie Palace. Orphelia recognized the building almost immediately—it was the Stone Shed.

Orphelia stood up and sat back down. Was she dreaming? Could this be true? It didn't seem possible. Yet there they were. Momma sat at a piano. She looked so young, and her hair was braided just like Orphelia's. Poppa had a big mustache and held a banjo. Uncle Winston, his head tilted, held a cornet. A tiny silver pin in the shape of a musical note, like the one he wore in his portrait back home, was on his jacket.

Poppa arrested? She'd never heard of such a thing! Poppa couldn't hurt a fly, let alone assault anybody. And this was how Uncle Winston had died? Dumped in the Mississippi and drowned? Or was he murdered first? Is that why Momma and Poppa didn't want to talk about him? Because he had been lynched?

The words whirled about in Orphelia's mind. Things had been confusing enough with so much silence around his death. Now all this other information—Poppa arrested, Momma and Poppa part of a musical trio—just made things even more mixed up.

Orphelia was about to bust with all these questions.

She felt a pang of loneliness for Pearl, who, for all her aggravating ways, had an answer for everything. Pearl would have found out from Momma about the music the Bruce Trio had played. Well, until she was with Pearl again, Orphelia would just have to sort out all this on her own.

She folded the newspaper back up and tucked it inside the songbook, behind the last page again. She looked out the window to where Laphet, Artimus, Bertha, Madame Meritta, and Othello stood in a loose-knit group. She bet they were discussing how to get across the river.

Orphelia wanted to run out and tell Madame about her discovery. But just then she noticed Reuben coming out of the storage wagon. He was carrying his pocket knife in one hand and a new, uncarved piece of wood in the other. He sat down on his bucket-chair a few yards away and began to whittle. Soon he was lost in his work.

This might be my only chance to do some investigating, thought Orphelia.

Madame Meritta had said that Reuben didn't have many belongings, but what he did have he kept in an old burlap sack in the storage wagon. Orphelia crept out of the coach quietly and made her way over to the wagon, keeping an eye on Reuben. He was busy carving away, humming his tuneless song.

Inside the wagon, she spotted the sack in a corner next to some barrels. Orphelia hesitated for a moment— she knew that snooping around in somebody else's personal property was wrong. Momma would switch her for sure if she ever found out. But it might be the only way she could ever learn anything that would explain all the strange things about Reuben. Orphelia opened up the sack and looked inside.

What she saw nearly made her faint with surprise. There were a few raggedy pieces of clothing, some crumpled-up playbills, his bowie knife, and an old hat, but mostly the bag was filled with wooden carvings — carvings that all looked exactly alike! She pulled one carefully out of the bag and turned it around in her hand, studying it. Reuben's handiwork was pretty rough, but she finally realized what it was supposed to be. It was a musical instrument. And not just any instrument — a cornet. The same instrument her uncle played. Reuben had been carving cornets. *But why?*

A noise outside made her jump. Was someone coming? Quickly she put the carving back in the sack, closed it up, and shoved it back into the corner where she'd found it. Then she waited. When she heard nothing more, she checked to make sure the coast was clear and then ducked out the door.

Orphelia went back to the sleeper coach, her head spinning. First the newspaper article, and now this. Why would Reuben carve cornets? She had never seen him play a real one, or any other instrument for that matter, and she couldn't imagine he was capable of such a thing anyway. It was clear he didn't have any musical talent. Poor man—even Pearl could carry a tune better than he could! Well, maybe Reuben just liked cornet music. Being around musical instruments all the time, he was bound to have a favorite one. Maybe he even wished he could be in Madame Meritta's band! *Not much chance of that,* thought Orphelia.

Then another idea came to her. If he liked cornet music so much, maybe he'd *always* loved it. Maybe he had been a fan of the Bruce Trio! That would explain how he knew Momma's name. He must have seen her parents perform! The thought of it made Orphelia giddy. If only Reuben could tell her what they had looked and sounded like. But according to Madame Meritta, Reuben couldn't even tell them his real name.

Where had Madame gone off to, anyway? She and the others were no longer standing around outside. Probably off rehearsing somewhere, Orphelia figured. Of course they didn't invite her. Why bother? She was going home soon.

Right now home didn't sound so bad, she had to admit. If she were at home, she'd be lying on her own comfortable bed and wearing clean stockings, and she wouldn't be hot and cramped. And wouldn't it be nice to take a bath in clean well water in their own washtub? She scratched her head. Were bugs living in her braids by now? Seemed like it had been ages since she'd washed her hair. When she left she hadn't thought to bring her comb and brush. Miss So-much-in-a-hurry!

"Madame Meritta, I have something to show you," Orphelia said that evening as they were getting ready for bed. Bertha was still at the campfire with some of the other musicians and wouldn't be coming in for a while. It was the first chance Orphelia had had to talk to Madame Meritta alone.

Orphelia reached into her schoolbag and pulled out the songbook with the newspaper clipping in the back of it. She hesitated. Momma had always warned against "putting family business in the street." That meant don't talk to people outside the family about family problems. Yet, their family problems had been in the newspaper, right on page one! Orphelia handed the clipping to Madame.

"Oh, my goodness." She gasped as she read the first paragraph. Her eyes got wider and wider. When she had finished the whole article, she took Orphelia's hand and squeezed it. "You poor thing. How awful for you and your family! But where did you get this?"

"I found it in the Stone Shed, with this songbook."

"The Stone Shed?"

"It's a run-down old building back in Calico Creek.

But I'm pretty sure it's what used to be the Dixie Palace."

"Well, I declare," Madame Meritta said, thumbing through the pages of the notebook. "That must be why your momma looked familiar to me."

Orphelia swallowed hard. "Momma never told me that she and Poppa were musicians and that they'd performed with Uncle Winston. And she never told me how he died, either. Why didn't she just tell me the truth?"

"All the more reason for you to get back home," said Madame, "so you can find out the answer. People have all kinds of reasons for keeping secrets. Imagine how sad your momma must have been to have a brother die that way, and then to never have a resting place for him where she could go to grieve and lay flowers or visit when the need arose."

Orphelia thought about that for a moment. Maybe that was the reason why Momma didn't like popular music any-more and didn't want Orphelia to, either.

And then an even deeper question raised itself. Was that why she didn't want Orphelia to be a performer? Because of what had happened to Uncle Winston?

༄

Early Monday morning, Orphelia woke to Bertha's hand shaking her shoulder. "Morning, sister. Good news! Laphet and them think they can drive the coaches to the other side by this afternoon. Water's already gone down enough that they don't think the horses will be scared."

Orphelia sat up, rubbing her eyes. *So why wake me up at the crack of dawn?* All she said was, "Yes, ma'am, that's good news."

"Which means if you got anything you want to wash, you'd best get up and start working on it now so that your clothes can get halfway dry before we have to get moving. Othello's got some grub cooking, but you better hurry 'cause he won't wait."

Orphelia wished she had brought along some white birch twigs to brush her teeth with. Maybe she could at least find some salt to rinse out her mouth. Orphelia pulled off her stockings and dug around in her schoolbag for her other clothes, but they were dirty, too. She stood up and examined her dress. It also needed to be washed, badly. She'd ask Madame Meritta what she could wear in the meantime.

Orphelia went outside into the cool morning. The sun was just beginning to make its climb into the sky, and dew lay thick on the grass.

Madame Meritta waved a pan of food at her from where she sat by the equipment wagon with a pile of clothes at her feet. "Rice and crawdaddies, courtesy of Othello. He said you loved it the other day."

Orphelia hesitated. "Uh, I ate it before I knew what it was," she said. She picked at the rice, separating the crayfish segments into a small pile by themselves. She was ready for some hominy and fatback about now, and a thick slab of Momma's johnnycake and some buttermilk.

"Orphelia, if you don't like it, you don't have to eat it," said Madame Meritta. "You can get some salted fish or beef out of the storage wagon."

"No, I can eat it," she said and jabbed a crayfish tail with her fork. She popped it in her mouth and chewed bravely. It wasn't bad, but she still couldn't get the picture out of her mind of the crayfish alive and wiggling, impaled on a fishing hook.

Madame Meritta handed her a cup of lye soap, a long shirt, and one of her skirts. "They're too big, but you can wear these while you're drying your dress."

Orphelia took the clothes and the soap, ducked back into the coach, and changed clothes. Then she followed Madame Meritta out a ways to a rocky outcropping near the water. "You have to do everything yourself?" said Orphelia.

"Everything except cook," said Madame Meritta. "I leave that to Othello."

Orphelia was soon busy washing her clothes, dipping them into the water, scrubbing them with lye soap, rinsing them, and with quick expert twists, wringing them out. Then, following Madame's example, she hung them on nearby branches to dry.

"You're pretty good," said Bertha as she came up

with an armload of men's clothing. "You think you can wash out Artimus's Sunday shirt for him? And Laphet's? Maryanne and I are doing their pants and other clothes. It'll be a big help for them, 'cause they're not real good at this kind of work."

Wanting to say "no" but not daring to, Orphelia nodded and began washing the shirts. The more shirts she washed, the more Bertha dropped off for her to do. The sun climbed higher in the sky. She wiped sweat off her forehead with her wrist. Her knees ached from having to lean on them against the rough rock, and her back felt like it was going to break.

Just when she thought she was finally finished, Reuben walked over and stood nearby, watching for a moment. Then he removed his ragged shirt and held it out. Orphelia stared at the shirt and then looked up at him.

"What?" she said. *Does he expect me to wash that filthy thing?* She turned to Madame Meritta for help, but Madame was nowhere to be found. Neither was Bertha.

"Can you wash my shirt?" Reuben asked. Beneath the one he had removed was another one, with even more holes.

"Can't you do it yourself?"

He bowed his head, clutching his shirt. He looked pitiful, with his shoulder bones sticking out through the holes. "Ain't no good at it."

"Oh all right. Give it here." Slowly and gingerly, she took the heavy woolen shirt. It was frayed at the collar and cuffs, with deep pockets on each side. And it smelled!

"Thankee," Reuben said. As he turned to go, something around his neck glittered in the sunlight. Orphelia noticed for the first time that he was wearing a tarnished silver chain around his neck, most of it hidden beneath his undershirt. Through one of the holes, a silver pendant peeked out. "Can I see your necklace?" she asked, curious about the pendant.

Reuben glowered.

"I know, I know, it's yours," Orphelia said, backing up a bit. "But I promise I won't even touch it. I just want to see it, is all. It's the least I deserve if I'm going to wash that grimy shirt of yours."

Reluctantly, Reuben pulled the chain out from under his shirt. Orphelia stood up on her toes and leaned forward to get a closer look at the pendant. A chill ran up and down her spine. It was shaped like a musical note — just like Uncle Winston's pin.

Right then Madame Meritta returned. "Reuben, could you go get some water for the horses?" Reuben nodded and headed back toward the coaches. "Orphelia, what's the matter with you? You look like you've seen a ghost. Reuben isn't still frightening you, is he?"

"No, ma'am," Orphelia said. "It's just that I was wondering where he might have gotten that pendant he has on that chain. My Uncle Winston had one like it, only his was a pin."

"Well, that is a funny coincidence, isn't it?" Madame Meritta said. "All I know is it was about the only thing he had on his person when we found him. It must be something very important to him. He never takes it off." She shrugged. "Now, why are we standing around talking about this when there's a heap of work yet to be done? Get yourself busy, young lady! We need to leave soon."

Madame Meritta instructed Orphelia to gather up all the dry clothes and bring them back to the camp. They had found a bridge about five miles downstream and wanted to get across before dark. "Artimus has gone ahead to telegraph your folks," explained Madame, "and let them know where you are. We'll catch up with Artimus in the town of Falsify, where we'll put you on the train for home."

Orphelia took the clothes off the branches, folded them carefully, and stacked them in piles. Carrying the clothes back to the coaches took two trips. She had just enough time to complete that chore before Madame Meritta called for her to help with something else. And all the while Orphelia was thinking, *Why does Reuben have a pendant just like my uncle's pin?* It had to be more than a coincidence. She was sure of it.

She almost bumped into Othello, who was carrying boxes from one coach to another.

"No time to daydream now, ma chère," he said as he moved out of her way, headed for the storage coach.

Orphelia hurried after him, remembering another question that had been weighing on her mind. "Mr. Othello, those men in Pitchfork Creek in the tent—were they going to lynch us 'cause we didn't put on blackface?" she asked.

Othello stopped and looked at her somberly. "Oh, no, no, no. Now listen to me, Orphelia. Lynching is a terrible, terrible thing, and it's true that our people have lost too many good men and women to murderers who hung them from trees, stoned them, beat them, and even threw their bodies in the river. But most people in Pitchfork Creek are good people, and the sheriff and his deputies were right there to protect us. So there's no need for you to let such thoughts cross your mind."

"Well, I just wondered." She looked after him as he rushed away. It was a relief to know that they wouldn't have been lynched. But then again, Uncle Winston had been in a jail with sheriff's deputies all around, and yet *he* had been lynched.

CHAPTER 8
A CRAZY IDEA

By sundown on Monday they had safely crossed the bridge. Reaching it took a lot longer than Othello had expected, however. It was on a winding narrow road that ran dangerously close to the streambed.

As they drove along, Orphelia half asleep, Othello and Madame Meritta discussed the pros and cons of whether to camp or to push on. Finally Madame told Othello to just stop wherever he could. He steered the sleeping coach as far to the side of the road as possible. Orphelia knew he was worried that if he left the path completely, the wagon would get stuck in the mud along the side of the road.

Orphelia huddled down in a corner of her sparse bed and gnawed on a strip of salted beef. The beef, which had never been tasty, was even less so now without Othello's touch. She wouldn't even have minded some of his crawdaddy gumbo. Her arms and back ached from the day's work. She slapped at mosquitoes and moths, scratched chigger bites, and sighed to herself.

Knowing everything she now knew about Momma and Uncle Winston, Orphelia realized that Madame Meritta was probably right about her parents being frantic with worry. Orphelia swallowed hard, a lump rising in her throat.

But on the other hand, how come they hadn't sent out the sheriff or anyone to find her and bring her home? Surely a search party would have caught up to the wagons by now. Maybe Momma and Poppa didn't care what happened to her. After all, Poppa had told her, "You've buttered your bread, now eat it." Was that what he was making her do now? She blinked away a tear. *I ran away, but I'm not a bad girl, not really. But maybe Momma thinks so by now.*

Bertha was squinting at a magazine in the dim light of the one kerosene lamp allowed in each coach. Madame Meritta sat cross-legged on her bed in her petticoats and undershirt. She was rubbing pomade into her thick black hair, which hung down past her shoulders.

"So how do you like show business on the road now?" Bertha asked Orphelia. She'd been watching Orphelia fight with the insects.

"Oh, I still like it." Orphelia sneezed. She scratched a chigger bite. She pulled at one of her braids. "I'm having a great adventure. Nobody else in Calico Creek has ever done anything like this before."

"You're probably right about that." Bertha rattled her magazine. "And when you get back home, you'll have another great adventure when your momma gets started on your behind."

"Bertha, don't tease her," said Madame Meritta. "Here, Orphelia, let me comb your hair and fresh up your braids." Madame Meritta scooted to the edge of her bed and patted it. "I can rub what I use into your hair, too, and help clean it without having to wash it. It's just castor oil and white wax with a little lemon oil. It smells good, too."

Orphelia gratefully crawled off her own bed and sat down on the floor, settling herself between the older woman's legs. Orphelia had wanted to wash her hair in the river today, but the laundry had kept her too busy.

Madame Meritta loosened both intertwined locks of Orphelia's hair and gently began scratching Orphelia's scalp with the edge of her comb. Next she parted Orphelia's hair and dabbed the sweet-smelling ointment along the part. When she had done this all over Orphelia's scalp, she placed more of the ointment in Orphelia's hair and rubbed vigorously.

"Mmmm, that feels good." Orphelia sighed like a cat purring. "Momma usually washes it on Saturday nights." Another lump formed in her throat at the thought of Momma. But this was real show business life now, she decided. The bad things like the riot and the awful food and the hard beds apparently were part of it, but having a famous person like Madame Meritta combing her hair as if they were old friends was really special. It was almost like home. Orphelia heard a whip'o'will call in the quiet, and another one answered it. That sounded like home, too.

The next thing Orphelia knew, she was waking up to the swaying of the wagon. It was daylight, and they were moving again. Orphelia yawned and stretched. Her arms were still sore from washing more clothes on Monday than she'd ever done at one time, even with Momma.

"Where are we?" Orphelia asked.

"Not too far from Falsify," replied Madame Meritta. Orphelia's heart sank.

But a few minutes later, the coach stopped. "Now what?" muttered Madame Meritta. "We still have two or three more miles to go." She got out to investigate. Orphelia followed, glad for the opportunity to stretch her legs. Othello, looking exasperated, stood next to the wagon talking to Artimus. What was Artimus doing back? Orphelia wondered. Weren't they supposed to meet him in Falsify?

"Bad news, Maryanne," said Artimus. "The train won't be running today. Seems that storm the other night flooded out part of the track."

Madame Meritta looked at Othello. "Tell me this isn't happening—*please*."

"I'm afraid so," he responded, sighing heavily.

"Orphelia, once again your stay with us seems to have been extended."

Orphelia could hardly believe her ears. "Does this mean what I think it means?" she asked breathlessly, her hands clasped with excitement. "Do I get to go to St. Louis with you after all?"

"Well, yes, it does look that way. If we stay in Falsify and wait, we won't make it to the fair in time, and we're not going to leave you here by yourself. It could be a day or so before the train is running again. So Artimus telegraphed your parents, asking them to meet us at Union Station in St. Louis. The tracks should be clear around these parts by the time your parents come through."

Orphelia was beside herself with happiness. *Oh, thank you, thank you, Lord!* She could easily put up with chiggers and mosquitoes and dried beef for a little longer if it meant she was going to see St. Louis. And was there still a chance that she might get to see the World's Fair, too?

That night Madame Meritta let Orphelia stay up a little longer at the campfire with the others. It was a beautiful spring evening, and after another long day on the road, Orphelia could hardly stand the thought of getting back into that stuffy coach again. And she was so excited about seeing St. Louis the next day that she didn't think she'd ever be able to fall asleep. But she also knew that the sooner she went to sleep, the sooner it would be morning. And the sooner it was morning, the sooner they would be on their way. Othello expected they'd reach St. Louis by tomorrow afternoon!

Orphelia yawned and excused herself to go to bed. Wearily she climbed up into the sleeper coach, more tired than she thought. Maybe the events of the past five days were finally catching up to her. She'd been on an adventure that she would never forget.

As excited as Orphelia was to reach St. Louis, a part of her didn't want the journey to end. And part of her also worried about seeing her folks. Orphelia shuddered to think of the punishment Momma would have come up with for her by now. She was probably boiling mad about having to go to St. Louis, on top of Orphelia running away. And what would happen when Orphelia told her parents what she knew about their past?

Orphelia reached into her schoolbag and pulled out the songbook with the article in it. She studied the book, wondering whose it might have been. She turned it over and, for the first time, noticed something written in tiny letters on the back cover, in the bottom right corner. When she looked closer, she saw they were somebody's initials — *W.T.*

Orphelia thought for a moment and then gasped. *W.T.? That stands for Winston Taylor!* Of course. This was

Uncle Winston's music. These were his own personal compositions and arrangements. He must have left the notebook behind the night of the riot! But how did the newspaper article get in the back of it? Maybe Momma or Poppa would know.

Poor Momma. What would she say when she saw her brother's songs after all these years? Would she be upset? Would she be angry? Would she be so shocked that she'd fly into some fit of hysterics like Reuben did when he heard "Lewis County Rag"?

Reuben . . .

A crazy idea began to form in Orphelia's head. And the more she thought about it, the crazier it got—and the crazier it got, the more it made sense.

Darting out of the coach into the darkness, Orphelia ran back to the campfire. "Madame Meritta!" she panted. "Back when you first found Reuben, what year did you say that was?"

Madame Meritta looked up at her in surprise. "Well, I don't remember exactly. It must have been about eleven or twelve years ago . . ."

"I remember," Othello piped up. "It was August of 1892. We were on our way back from Iowa, yes? Camped near the river somewhere. But why do you want to know, Orphelia?"

"Oh, just curious!" She ran back to the coach, her heart pounding and her hands trembling as she pulled the newspaper article out of the back of the notebook. She unfolded it. The newspaper was dated August 8, 1892, just as she'd thought.

Scanning down to the bottom of the article, Orphelia read the last sentence. "Sheriff's officials say that although the body has not been found, Taylor is presumed dead."

Presumed dead, Orphelia repeated to herself. *Presumed.* But maybe Uncle Winston wasn't dead after all. Maybe Uncle Winston was . . . Reuben.

It hardly seemed possible, and yet it made perfect sense. Madame Meritta had found Reuben that same August, downriver from where Uncle Winston had been thrown in the Mississippi. The lynching and near-drowning would have left Uncle Winston's head so scrambled up that he couldn't remember who he was, but surely some memories could have survived, tucked way down deep inside him. That's what must have come bubbling up when Orphelia played "Lewis County Rag." After all, it was his own composition he was hearing! And of course Orphelia would have reminded him of Momma, his sister. The ruckus in Pitchfork Creek must have jarred his memory and made him relive that terrible night at the Dixie Palace. And even if his brain didn't work well enough anymore to be able to sing or play music, or even remember anything else about his previous life, some part of his mind still hung on to that old self, carving all those wooden cornets.

And the silver musical note—well, the only thing that didn't make sense was why Reuben's was a pendant and not a pin, but surely there was an explanation for that. She would just have to figure out what it was.

But how? Until she could think of a way to prove her theory about Reuben, she would have to keep it a secret. It was too big a pronouncement to make based on a hunch. She would just get in trouble for talking nonsense and agitating people with her crazy notions. Better to wait till she was absolutely, positively sure. But it would have to be soon. She didn't have much time left, with Madame Meritta's Marvelous Traveling Troubadours approaching St. Louis.

Madame Meritta was smiling and walking from one side of the swaying coach to the other, picking up clothing and boxes and moving them back and forth. The midday sun was already high in the sky, and they were nearing the outskirts of the city.

"I can't wait to get home. I live just off Market Street, not far from Union Station. I can't wait to get to my own bed and my own kitchen, my own little house! Sometimes this coach gives me so much claustrophobia that I could scream!"

"So I'll get to see your house?" Orphelia asked, trying to disguise the hope in her voice.

"It depends on the time we get into town and what train your parents will be arriving on. Artimus instructed them to send a telegram, letting us know when to expect them, so we need to check on that first. But let's not talk about that now. Look! Look outside!"

Orphelia crawled over to the window. What she saw made her open her mouth and close it. She turned to Madame Meritta, then back to the window in astonishment. "Why, I've never seen so many mules and horses together! Is this a rodeo or something?"

"Not exactly. They're being herded to the World's Fair." The coaches had stopped at an intersection of a road that crossed the railroad tracks not far from the Mississippi River. The animals had just been unloaded from a long string of brightly decorated boxcars that said *Boer War Reenactment Exhibit.* "Look over there at that steamboat on the water," Madame said, pointing.

The steamboat, she explained, had returned from being anchored near Hannibal. It held huge fish tanks for Illinois's state fish exhibit at the fair.

"Miz Madame, I hope this doesn't sound sassy, but Momma said she heard that our people weren't being treated right at the fair. Is that true?"

Madame Meritta rubbed her chin and folded her arms. "I wish I could have answered that question directly to your mother. Let's just say that I'm positive our people will get a better shake here than we did at the Chicago

World's Fair. At least that's what the *Palladium* would have us believe."

"What's the *Palladium*?"

"It's one of our colored newspapers. We have colored hotels, colored restaurants, colored photographers — everything! We have ragtime musicians pouring in from everywhere to play at our clubs and get noticed. There's a fella here named Tom Turpin who owns the Rosebud Saloon on Market Street. He's writing a song called 'St. Louis Rag.' Before this fair is over in December, every-body'll have that song on their lips! But the World's Fair board won't let anybody play ragtime on any official pro-gram because it says ragtime's not respectable. Shoot, that's not stopping our fellas. They're getting music jobs on the Pike and playing ragtime there to big crowds. We'll be playing on the Pike, too. That's the big mile-long mid-way just outside the gates, you know. It's part of the fair, but you can get in for free."

As Madame Meritta explained that Negro businesses and clubs planned to put up displays at the fair demon-strating the accomplishments of the Negro, she was walk-ing back and forth and waving her arms around. Orphelia hadn't seen her this excited before.

"This way the city and the big white business owners and other fair-goers will see that Negroes are respectable, smart, and able to do most anything when given the chance. Then maybe we can get the kinds of jobs that will help us elevate ourselves and gain more economic and political leadership in city government."

She added that the city had spent a lot of money fixing up some of the neighborhoods. On her street they planted new trees and got gas streetlights. The city also tore down a lot of old, ramshackle tenement houses and cleared empty lots of overgrown weeds and garbage.

"I guess Momma would be surprised to hear all that," Orphelia said. Sounded like Momma was wrong again.

The closer Madame Meritta's entourage got to St. Louis, the more crowded the roads became. Now Orphelia was seeing throngs of people in horse-drawn wagons, with suitcases and children piled in the back. Orphelia glued her face to the window, taking in every detail so she could remember to tell Pearl about it all.

A short time later, they had reached the city itself. Motorcars, puttering and smoking, threaded through the streets around horses and bicycles. Children who looked like Orphelia played in the streets or sat on porches attached to houses three and four stories high. Mothers with babies in one arm and laundry baskets in the other chatted with one another. Men shined shoes on street corners or in small cubbyholes by stores, pushed cartloads of fruits and vegetables, or washed windows.

And just off in the distance were the grounds of the Louisiana Purchase Exhibition—the St. Louis World's Fair. Orphelia could see the magnificent giant Ferris wheel

looming off to the left. She sighed. She was so close to
the fair, and yet so far away.

And she still hadn't thought of any way to prove her
theory about Reuben. Time was running out. If Orphelia
didn't think of something fast, the chance of reuniting
Momma and Poppa with Uncle Winston might be gone
forever.

Unless . . . Maybe Orphelia didn't need any proof.
Maybe all she needed was to get Momma to meet Reuben
somehow. Surely Momma would recognize her own
brother, even after all these years, no matter how much
he'd changed. She would be able to see past the scarred
face and the one eye that was swollen shut. Orphelia
wouldn't need any more proof than that when she told
Momma and Poppa her theory.

But what if Momma *didn't* recognize him? Orphelia
would be in even bigger trouble than ever, stirring up
memories of Uncle Winston like that and meddling in the
affairs of adults. *Maybe I should just mind my own business.
Momma and Poppa probably won't even show up anyway.*

Othello spoke through the driver's hole. "Train station's just a few blocks further. Laphet and the others
are heading off now. Artimus is going to the telegraph
office. He'll meet us back at the station."

Did that mean Reuben was gone, too? A knot twisted
in Orphelia's stomach, and her heart flip-flopped. "Miz
Madame, I don't feel well," she said.

"Then lie down. I'll pour you some water so you can freshen up here." She touched Orphelia's forehead, then gently lay her palm on her cheek. "You're not overly warm. I know you've been dreading the end of your great adventure. And you know what? I've been dreading it, too. I surely have, but the time has come for you to go back home. You've gotten much farther than either one of us expected, you know."

Orphelia pressed her face against Madame Meritta's skirt. Her throat grew so full that she could barely talk. Tears rolled out the corners of her eyes and stained the skirt. "I don't want to say good-bye to you, Madame Meritta! Or Mr. Othello either!"

"Oh, Orphelia, Orphelia." Madame softly rubbed her back and shoulder. "You've become very special to me, too, much as I hate to admit it. This is the first time since my son—" Her eyes filled with tears. She paused, and then cleared her throat and continued. "Well, it's been just wonderful to have you with us these past few days. But you're not our child, Orphelia. You belong with your own family. There's a hole in your home with you gone," Madame Meritta said. "I know what it's like not to have my child around, believe me. Your parents and your sister are in a lot of pain."

"Well, if that's true, then why didn't they try to find me?"

"How do you know they didn't?"

"They probably won't even come to St. Louis. Momma hates it, and she probably hates *me* so much that she never wants to see me again."

Madame lifted Orphelia up by the shoulders. "I promise you that is not true. Now stand up. Wash your face and get ready to go."

CHAPTER 9

ORPHELIA'S LAST CHANCE

Orphelia stumbled over to the water basin and washed her tear-salty face. She glanced again out the window at the masses of people, animals, and trolleys traveling through the big city's streets. Was this really the end? Despite her earlier homesickness, she still wanted to see St. Louis. And she wanted to find out if Reuben was her Uncle Winston. And most important, she still wanted to sing at the Fair.

Maybe she could run away again. *I'll fly into a crowd of folks and disappear so fast nobody'll catch me. Doesn't matter that I don't have a penny to my name or a mud hole to sleep in, as Cap would say. I ran away once before, and I can do it again!*

But the thought of being alone in a city as huge as this one made little quiverings in her stomach. "I bet a person could get lost easy in St. Louis," Orphelia said.

"Yes, if nobody was holding her hand tightly,"
Madame Meritta answered quietly. "And if she did get
lost, it would be an awful thing. There's probably lots of
murderers and thieves and other kinds of ruffians in
town right now that a lost young girl would not want to
run into."

A chill went down Orphelia's back. She swallowed
and dried her face. Then she set her chin on the palm of
her hand and stared out of the window. Soon she noticed
a tall, pointy clock tower sticking up over the rooftops.
It looked like it was part of a magnificent castle. A short
time later, she saw the castle itself.

"That's the train station," Madame Meritta said,
pointing to the gigantic structure.

Orphelia gasped. This was the *train station*? It was
nothing like any train station she'd ever seen. Most of
the ones she'd been in weren't more than a one- or two-
room building next to a platform.

Othello pulled the coach up to the curb, and
Madame Meritta stepped out. Orphelia stayed where
she was until Madame reached in and waggled her finger
at her. "Orphelia Bruce, don't make me have to come
back in that coach and pull you out by the ear."

"Oh all right, I'm coming." Orphelia sighed. For once
she dreaded having to leave the coach, but she told herself
that at least she would get to see the inside of the train
station. She slipped the strap of her schoolbag around her

neck and stepped down. The odor of burnt coal and wood, thick in the air, made her cough.

With Madame Meritta tightly holding her right hand and Othello firmly holding her left, they headed into the station. Orphelia gaped in wonder as they entered the huge stone building. A sea of people, most of them probably fair-goers, rushed by in every direction.

Othello disappeared into the crowd to see about train schedules and to meet up with Artimus. Madame Meritta and Orphelia found a bench near the ticket counter and sat down to wait. Orphelia was surprised to learn that there was no separate waiting room for colored people. In any other train station she'd ever been in, Negroes had to sit in broken-down benches in a side room or off in a corner, and there was maybe a pail of dingy water with a leaky tin cup for them to drink from. Madame explained that Union Station was one of the few public places in St. Louis that wasn't segregated.

When Othello finally reappeared, he was frowning.

"Oh, no. What is it now?" asked Madame Meritta.

"They're not coming, are they?" said Orphelia. "See?"

"Nonsense, child," replied Othello. "They are coming. The message says that they will be arriving on the 7:30 P.M. train."

Orphelia's heart fluttered. The shock of knowing she would be seeing her parents soon both exhilarated and horrified her.

"But there was another telegram waiting for us, too, Maryanne," continued Othello. "Our performance date has been moved up. We've got to perform tonight, at eight o'clock. Now don't get upset, my dear. We can't complain too much. I had to negotiate for hours to get us booked in the first place because competition was so stiff. After all, the Show-Me Café's a popular place."

"Well, I declare, could anything else possibly go wrong?" Madame Meritta asked, sighing heavily. "I just hope enough of my musicians are in town." She pulled out her watch chain and checked the time. "It's almost four. We can drive around and round up as many folks as possible."

Cautiously Orphelia crossed her fingers. Maybe she would have a chance to perform at the fair after all. "What about the talent show performance? The Hannibal Twins can't get here from Hannibal by then. So can I be—"

"No, you can't substitute for the Twins," Madame Meritta snapped back.

"But how are you going to find all your musicians in time? And who'll replace Orville, the Musical Orphan Boy?"

Orphelia saw fire blaze briefly in the older woman's eyes. "I'll just go with whatever I've got. Now stop asking questions."

"Maryanne," Othello said, "Artimus also informed

me that Pittsburgh and Becker have left to join some other dance group. Can you imagine such infidelity? So we now have two more holes to fill."

"What? How could they double-cross us like that?" Madame Meritta got so frowned up that a crumple of hair fell down in her face from under her hat. "It's the money—well, I mean, *no* money."

Orphelia couldn't believe her luck. "Madame Meritta, now you *really* need me. You gotta have a featured act," she said. "Please, please, please let me perform tonight with you all. I was Orville the Musical Orphan Boy only once, and I didn't get to take all my bows and leave the stage like a real performer. Just give me that one chance. We can leave a message for my parents telling them to meet us at the—"

"I said be quiet!" Madame Meritta snarled.

Orphelia closed her mouth and looked away.

Othello touched Madame Meritta on the arm. "Time is escaping, Madame. Even if we don't allow the child to be in the show, what are we to do with her right now? We can't leave her here alone, and we must hurry if we're to round everyone up and be ready to perform by eight."

Orphelia held her breath.

Finally, Madame Meritta threw her hands in the air. "Okay, I give up. Orphelia, I don't want to get any more involved in something that your parents are already in a trauma over, but it's true that they wouldn't want us to leave you by yourself in a place like this. You'll have to stay with us. But you are *not* going to perform tonight, do you understand me?"

"Yes, ma'am," Orphelia said, trying to hide her excitement. There was still a chance. She was sure of it.

CHAPTER 10

THE GRAND FINALE

Shortly after seven o'clock Madame Meritta and her entourage, including an overjoyed Orphelia, arrived at the Show-Me Café in the mile-long amusement zone called the Pike. The excitement Orphelia had felt when she first entered St. Louis was nothing compared to her amazement when she reached the Pike.

It was packed with more people than Orphelia had ever seen before, people from all around the world. They wore long gowns, brightly colored shirts and skirts and pants, and turbans and caps. Their skins were pale, red, yellow, brown, and black.

Orphelia was itching to explore. The coaches were parked beside the café, and Madame Meritta was busy getting herself ready for the show. Othello and the others were unloading the equipment wagon. When Orphelia was sure no one was watching, she darted off into the crowd. She wouldn't go very far; she had to be back in plenty of time to carry out a plan that had been forming in her head since they left the train station.

Orphelia wandered around, marveling at the sights. There were huge statues, castles, and temples built to resemble those found in places around the world, from France and Spain to Egypt to the continent of Asia. There were Eskimo igloos and even a reproduction of the high peaks of the Alps towering over a Swiss mountain village. She gawked at all the exhibit halls and at the people in the crowd.

Orphelia had read in newspapers at school that the St. Louis World's Fair was so spectacular that visitors with health problems were told to be very careful lest they be overwhelmed and fall ill. Though Orphelia hadn't become ill, she felt like she had stepped into another world completely.

There were wild and trained animals in cages—water buffalo, dogs, lions, and bears. There was even an enormous elephant, part of the magnificent Hagenbeck's Animal Show.

Suddenly the elephant lifted its trunk, opened its mouth, and bellowed so loudly that Orphelia's teeth vibrated. Staring in amazement, she stumbled backward and bumped right into a white woman with two babies in her arms.

"Oh, sorry," Orphelia said.

The woman looked at her and curled her lip. "Dirty little tramp," she snapped. "Stay out of my way, you hear? Your kind don't belong here."

Orphelia looked down at her clothing. After six days on the road, she did look pretty raggedy—like a common gutter girl, as Momma would say. Even so, the woman didn't need to talk so hateful to her, she thought angrily. Maybe this was what Momma meant when she said colored people wouldn't get treated nice at the fair.

"Hi ya, missy," a white man at a food booth called out to Orphelia as she passed. "Have one! Best-tasting food in America! Just like they fix 'em at the ballpark." He waved her over and handed her a cylinder-shaped piece of meat wrapped in a blanket of bread. "Take it, it's a free sample," he said cheerfully.

Orphelia took the food and sniffed it. It looked like one of the fat sausage links that Momma made when she squeezed ground pork into skin casings at pig-killing time. Orphelia took a bite and was relieved that it was good. "Thanks, mister," she said.

"That's a hot dog, in case you didn't know," the man explained as he handed samples to other passersby. "It's gonna be everybody's number one food in the world one of these days."

As Orphelia walked around, she thought about the meanness of the woman with the babies compared to the kindness of the food vendor. Madame Meritta and

Momma had both been right. Orphelia might as well expect to get treated mean one time and nice another. It was just like being back home.

A large clock in the shape of the state of Missouri showed that it was almost seven-thirty. She gobbled down the hot dog and ran back to the café.

Madame Meritta stood waiting for her, her right toe tapping furiously and her arms folded across her chest. Her face was so pinched up she looked like she was about to explode.

"Orphelia, where on earth have you been?! Are you crazy, running off by yourself like that? Lord knows I got plenty of other things to be doing right now than worrying about your whereabouts! Now get in that coach and stay there, and don't even think about coming out till I say so! You can forget about watching the show."

Normally Orphelia would have been devastated by those words, but right now they were just what she wanted to hear. Her plan would be easier to carry out this way. Now she could remain in the coach while everyone else was inside the café, instead of having to sneak out during the show. She retreated to the coach, secretly celebrating her good luck.

Madame Meritta came in to finish putting on her makeup. Orphelia watched her silently. She wished she wasn't about to disobey the older woman again. Madame had been so kind to her, and Orphelia hated to cause her any more grief.

At last Othello arrived to escort Madame Meritta backstage. "Madame, it's just about time to make our entrance," he called from outside.

"I'll come back for you when the performance is over," Madame said stiffly to Orphelia. Then, her face softening a bit, she added, "I'll bring your parents with me. By now their train should have arrived and they should be on their way to the café."

Her parents! Orphelia's heart skipped a beat. What if they didn't arive on time? What if they *did?* She couldn't decide which would be worse.

Orphelia's Orphan Boy costume still hung from the same ceiling hook where she had placed it after Pitchfork Creek. As soon as Madame was gone, Orphelia changed into the costume and tucked her hair under her hat. She fished the songbook out of her schoolbag and stuffed it into the top of her baggy trousers, covering it with the loose-fitting shirt.

Orphelia heard the opening notes of Madame Meritta's Marvelous Traveling Troubadours' theme song floating out of the Show-Me Café. That was her cue. *Now is the time and this definitely is the place. No matter what happens,* she told herself, *at least I tried.*

She left the coach and went around to the front entrance of the café. The doorman looked at her baggy clothes strangely, but when she told him she was with the show, he nodded. Breathing a sigh of relief, she went in.

Her heart beat excitedly as she made her way to the back of the theater and stood in the shadows just like she had in Pitchfork Creek.

The electric lights flickered merrily above her like stars shining in a purple sky. A candelabra chandelier above the stage grew brighter until every light blazed. Othello strode out to the edge of the stage in his white derby hat and white cutaway coat and tails. He tipped his hat, smiling at the audience, and introduced himself as the Great Grand Master.

Orphelia swallowed nervously. How would she get onstage? Were Momma and Poppa out there already? What would they do when they saw her? What if, after finally realizing her dream of performing at the World's Fair, she was a failure? What if the audience booed her?

Othello introduced Madame Meritta, who floated out in a golden gown with sparkly jewelry around her neck and wrists and a gigantic tiara on her head. Her hair hung down past her shoulders. What a beautiful lady she was! When she began to sing a song about St. Louis, the audience applauded. The more she sang, the more they applauded. By the end of the song the audience was on its feet cheering. So was Orphelia.

Next came two men and two women dancing a fancy

cakewalk. They must have been some of Madame's St. Louis backup performers, because Orphelia didn't recognize any of them.

Orphelia patted her foot and pretended to dance with them. During the next acts, she concentrated on practicing the words to her songs and rehearsing the fingering in her head.

The show neared its end. Sweating in the heavy clothing, Orphelia ignored the butterflies in her stomach. It was time to make her move. Otherwise, the show would be over and so would her dream.

Othello came to the stage again and began to thank the audience and café owners while the band softly played its theme song.

Orphelia straightened her hat. She rushed toward the stage, but she immediately discovered that it wasn't as easy speeding around tables and chairs as it had been to run up the aisle in Pitchfork Creek. She bumped into a chair and fell into a woman's lap.

"I'm sorry, I'm sorry," she said, getting up. She careened against a table and fell to the floor. Still on her knees, she waved her hand. "Mr. Great Grand Master, Mr. Grand Master, I'm back again like I promised. Don't forget me!"

Othello paused and looked around. "Turn up the houselights, please," he said. "Who is calling the Great Grand Master?"

As the lights came up, Orphelia struggled to her feet and caught Othello's eye. "It's me—Orville, your Musical Orphan Boy. I'm back! Don't forget me!"

"Orville?" Othello said, his face full of surprise.

People began to chuckle and point at her. Orphelia made it to the edge of the stage. She tugged at Othello's pants leg. "Oh, please, Mr. Great Grand Master, please let me sing my song of sorrow!"

Letting go of his pants leg, she slipped down on one knee and held her arms out wide. "Just give me my one last chance."

"Ladies and gentlemen, a moment, please," said Othello. He bent down to her and whispered, "You just don't give up, do you, Orphelia?" He stood up, removed his derby, and tapped his head with one thick forefinger, appearing to be deep in thought.

Orphelia began to sing softly. She rose to a full standing position, singing louder and louder. She stopped singing, then clutched her hands together and raised them in the air toward Othello.

Following his gaze to the left, Orphelia saw, right in the front row, Momma, Poppa—and Pearl! They were all there, staring at Orphelia in shock. Seeing her family after nearly a week's absence made Orphelia lose her concentration for a few seconds, but she regained it and continued singing.

Othello smiled a little, then broke out into a grandiose

grin. Bowing to her, he helped Orphelia up onstage.

"Ladies and gentlemen, I bring you our little Orville, who will capture your hearts. Please prepare yourselves with handkerchiefs. And now . . . Orville, our Musical Orphan Boy Prodigy!"

Orphelia bowed to the audience and struck a pose. She began to sing "Homeless Child," then abruptly remembered that she was supposed to be playing the piano. Still singing, she slipped over to the band at the front of the stage. The piano player stood up and gave her his seat.

People in the audience began to nod and dab at their eyes as she sang. When she gained enough courage, she glanced down at her family. Poppa sat with a proud smile on his face; Pearl was grinning and waving; and Momma—well, Momma looked like she had turned to stone.

At the end of the song Orphelia stood up and bowed. The audience stood, too, clapping heartily. Thrilled by the response, Orphelia sat back down at the piano. She glanced at Othello, who nodded and tipped his hat to her. "Isn't she divine? Orville, our Musical Orphan Boy Prodigy! Or should I say Miss Orville, our Musical Orphan *Girl* Prodigy! Perhaps she'll give us one more song."

Orphelia sang and played "Listen to the Mocking-bird," which the audience loved as well. Then Othello started for the center of the stage, signaling her to finish.

But Orphelia wasn't about to stop now. She broke into "Lewis County Rag."

The audience clapped in time to the song, and people waved their hats. Orphelia looked over at her parents. Poppa's mouth had fallen open. Momma pressed her hands to her face.

Quickly Orphelia ended the song and stood up. The applause was thunderous. Orphelia jumped off the stage and ran to her family as the crowd began to file out.

Poppa placed his hands on her shoulders and then took her into his arms. "I'm so glad you're still in one piece, Li'l Sweets."

Pearl clamored to hug her, too. "Everybody at school and church has been talking up a storm about you," she whispered. "Momma refused to go to St. Louis, even after we got that second telegram. But I told her if we didn't go, I'd run away, too. So, see? I promised I'd make it up to you."

Momma stood back, her mouth a straight line across her face. Poppa and Pearl moved a little to one side. Orphelia forced herself to look up. "Hello, Momma," she said softly.

"Orphelia," Momma said, her voice as cold as ice, "where did you learn that song?"

"Otisteen, can't you say hello first?" Poppa broke in. He put his arm around Orphelia. "She's here, she's all right, and she's just shown us what a bundle of talent she has. Orphelia, I'm sorry you had to run away to make us see how much you love music."

"It's okay, Poppa. I learned the song from this, Momma," Orphelia said, pulling the composition book out of her trousers. "I found it in the Stone Shed. It was Uncle Winston's, wasn't it?"

Momma gasped and raised one hand to her mouth.

Orphelia continued. "I know now why you didn't want me to perform. I know all about how you and Poppa and Uncle Winston were playing at the Dixie Palace. And I know how Uncle Winston got killed—only I'm not really sure he's dead—but I read about the lynching in this article." Orphelia pulled out the newspaper page, unfolded it, and held it up.

"What is it? Let me see!" Pearl snatched the newsprint out of Orphelia's hand.

Momma began to sob and fell against Poppa's chest. He held her tightly.

"So you found it, Orphelia," he said quietly.

"Great grumpity gracious! This really happened?" Pearl shouted out as she read the article. "How come I don't remember any of it?"

"Because you were only a baby then, Pearl. Too young to know what was going on," Poppa explained.

"But, Poppa, why didn't you just tell us about it?" asked Orphelia.

"We could never agree on when we should," Momma

spoke up. "I always blamed myself for what happened, because I was the one who wanted to have a trio." Othello brought a chair over for Momma to sit down on. "If I hadn't been so insistent, Winston would have never joined. He loved to play and compose, but not professionally. He just wanted to be a farmer. *I* wanted us to travel and perform. Just when it seemed that we were getting popular, this terrible thing happened."

Momma looked down at her hands. Then she looked up at Orphelia and shook her head. "You see, I thought if I kept you from playing sassy music that you'd be safe and that you wouldn't want to follow in my footsteps. You are so much like me, Orphelia, and I was afraid. Oh, I've known for years that Pearl's not a musician, so I never worried about her. But you?" She sighed and fumbled at her throat with trembling fingers. "I just was so afraid. I didn't want to lose you, too."

Orphelia searched Momma's face. "Momma, do you hate me now? Are you going to say I can't play piano anymore when we get back home?"

"No, Orphelia. You have too much of a gift for me to make you keep it to yourself."

Orphelia could barely keep herself from jumping with elation. She threw her arms around her mother's neck. "Oh, thank you, Momma! Does this mean I can play whatever kind of music I like from now on?"

"Yes—well, *almost* any kind. But first we have to get

you back home. And don't think you won't be punished for all this!" Momma scolded, sounding more like herself again. "You disobeyed us. I didn't raise girls to lower themselves and act like common gutter girls. You're wearing boy's clothes! Proper young Negro women don't cavort in public in men's trousers."

"Yes, ma'am," Orphelia said, stifling a giggle. Some things about Momma would never change. But Orphelia didn't mind. It was comforting in a way.

Madame Meritta approached. "I can assure you, Miz Bruce, that it was never my intention for your daughter to hook up with our show when we left Calico Creek," she said. "I nearly had a spasm when I discovered her in our storage coach. But she truly has been a joy, so tidy, so hardworking, that she really wasn't much trouble. But I am glad to hand her back over to you."

Momma blew her nose into a handkerchief. "I can't thank you enough for taking care of her these last few days. It's a relief to know my daughter was in such responsible hands the whole time."

Pearl spoke up just then. "Orphelia, what did you mean when you said you weren't sure that Uncle Winston was dead?"

"I'm sure she just wants to believe there's still a chance he's alive," said Poppa, "just like we did. It was so painful for us because we never found his body. But he is gone, Orphelia. We finally accepted it, and you must too."

Out of the corner of her eye, Orphelia saw Reuben creep to the side of the stage. He was staring at Momma and Poppa. "Well, it's just that—" she started.

"Who is that man?" Momma asked, frowning.

"Oh, that's Reuben," replied Madame Meritta. "Sort of a hired hand. Well, more like 'found' hand, in this case."

This was Orphelia's chance. "Momma, Poppa, I think he's someone you all should meet." She went over to Reuben, took him by the hand, and led him over to her parents. "He was found about half dead by the river, somewhere south of Hannibal, right after Uncle Winston was lynched. He can't remember anything about where he came from or what happened to him, but, Momma, one time he called me by your name."

"Orphelia, what are you trying to say?" said Poppa.

"Reuben, can I see that pendant you have on that chain around your neck?" Orphelia asked. Reuben shook his head no and nervously backed away.

"Please, Reuben?" she asked again softly. "It's really important. I promise nothing bad will happen to it."

Reluctantly he pulled the chain out from under his shirt. The silver musical note dangled from it, catching the glow of the stage lights.

Momma leaned slightly forward and looked at it. Then she looked at Reuben. Then her eyes got large, and she fainted.

While Poppa attended to Momma, Madame Meritta

demanded to know what was going on. "Orphelia, what's all this got to do with Reuben?"

"Miz Madame," Orphelia said. "You all might call him Reuben, but my family calls him Uncle Winston."

❧

Later that evening, Orphelia and Pearl sat on the ornate couch in Madame Meritta's parlor while the adults talked about Reuben—Uncle Winston. Madame had just brought in a tray of lemon tarts and iced tea for everyone. Momma rested on another couch with a wet cloth on her forehead, and Poppa sat nearby. Othello and Reuben were outside tending to the horses.

Even after everything had been explained to Reuben, he still didn't really know who he was or that he was with his family. But that wasn't important, Momma said. What mattered most was that he was still alive.

"Much as we hate to part with him again," Poppa was saying to Madame Meritta, "we think he should stay here with you all. It may take quite a while before he understands who we are—if he ever does. Poor fella's been through a lot, but he's happy now. And I assure you we will help out in any way we can to make sure he's not a financial burden to you."

The fact that Orphelia had solved the mystery surrounding the whereabouts of her missing uncle had not quite hit home yet. All she could really think about was that Momma didn't hate her after all, and that she could keep playing the piano.

"Girl, Cap was going on and on about how he gave you instructions on what to do on the road," Pearl told her. "Miz Rutherford's face was so long it looked like somebody had run over her with a motorcar. Now you're going to have to tell me every single thing that you saw, did, smelled, touched, heard, tasted—"

"I had to wash clothes and scrub floors is what I did," Orphelia said. "It's hard work traveling around like that. I got a crimp in my back from sleeping in that little bed in the coach, and if I never eat another piece of salted beef ever again, that'll be all right with me. I thought being in a traveling show would be all music and pretty clothes and somebody else cooking all your meals, but it's not."

"So you're ready to go back home now?" Momma said.

"Well, maybe just for a little while." Orphelia smiled sheepishly.

Then Orphelia remembered to ask Momma the story behind Uncle Winston's pin.

"It was a gift from our father, you see, and it was Uncle Winston's good-luck charm. But your uncle had a habit of losing things," Momma recalled with a smile, "and so a short time after that portrait was taken, he decided to have the pin put on a chain that he could wear around his neck. He never took it off after that."

Then Poppa explained to Orphelia that what she'd read in the newspaper was not quite how the Dixie Palace riot had occurred.

"The man in the Dixie Palace—yes, that was the Stone Shed—actually grabbed up a handful of ashes from the fireplace and tried to rub it on your mother's face," said Poppa, shaking his head. "He was drunk, of course. And naturally, Winston and I tried to protect her. The fella lost his balance and hit his head on the edge of a table. But times being what they were, with so many lynchings going on around the South and Midwest, why, it didn't take much for mob mentality to take over."

"I still can't believe that happened in our own Lewis County." Orphelia shuddered. "I always thought it was a good place to live."

"It is, Orphelia. That drunk who started the trouble and his devilish buddies were not even from Lewis County," Poppa said, putting a hand on Orphelia's shoulder. "Lewis County is a good place to live."

"But, Poppa," Pearl piped up, "there's something I still don't understand. How did Uncle Winston's composition book end up in the piano bench in the Stone Shed, with the newspaper article in it?"

"Yes, Thelton, that's a good question," said Momma, propping herself up on her elbows. "You were supposed to destroy it, remember? I didn't want any reminders left of that horrible night."

"I know," said Poppa. "But I thought there might come a day when you'd change your mind and regret not having held on to your brother's music. Those compositions were one-of-a-kind. So I stuck the newspaper article in the back of the composition book and hid them both in the piano bench."

"Good thing you did, too, or Orphelia would never have found Uncle Winston!" said Pearl.

"Yes, I suppose that's true," Momma admitted. "Thank you, Thelton. I realize now that I should have kept that songbook anyway and learned to play all those songs myself, in his memory. But instead, I haven't touched a piano since."

"Maybe now you'll start playing again," Orphelia said. "Is that old piano in the Stone Shed yours?"

"Oh, no. After that awful night, I gave my piano to the church. You've been playing on it all this time, Orphelia."

Orphelia smiled so hard she thought her lips would split. "Maybe that's why I love it so much."

1904

A Peek into the Past

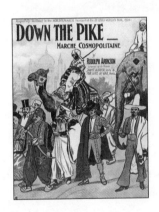

The main street of a small Missouri town around 1900

In 1904, small-town life in Missouri had changed little since the end of the Civil War nearly 40 years before. People still traveled mostly by foot or on wagons drawn by mules or horses. Few buildings had indoor plumbing or electricity. A girl Orphelia's age would probably never have traveled beyond her hometown or seen big-city sights like an automobile or a theater.

In black communities like Calico Creek, people's lives centered around the church. For a musically inclined girl like Orphelia, the church offered a chance to get training in piano and voice—and to perform before the congregation every Sunday.

A visit by a traveling minstrel show would have been a rare and thrilling event, and most of the town would have turned out to see it. A traditional minstrel show always began with the whole troupe singing onstage as

ALG. FIELD GREATER MINSTRELS

OLDEST, BIGGEST, BEST

DOC QUIGLEYS

LATEST CREATION THE D...

the curtain rose. Next came singing, dancing, and comedy acts. Each act was introduced by the *interlocutor,* or announcer.

In Orphelia's day, both white and black audiences enjoyed minstrel songs, which portrayed the lives of southern black people, often in a humorous or romantic way. Audiences also loved dances like the cakewalk, which featured jaunty strutting and fancy footwork.

Before the Civil War, minstrel shows featured white performers who mimicked the speech and music of black slaves to entertain white audiences. The performers dressed in tattered clothes and smeared their faces with burnt cork, or *blackface* makeup. After slavery was outlawed, many white Southerners felt bitter toward the former slaves, and their imitation of blacks in minstrel shows became even more

insulting. White minstrel show managers began to hire black singers and dancers but made them wear the exaggerated blackface makeup too, because that was what white audiences expected to see.

Black performers found putting on blackface disturbing, but they had little choice if they wanted to keep

By the late 1800s, minstrel shows often featured black performers.

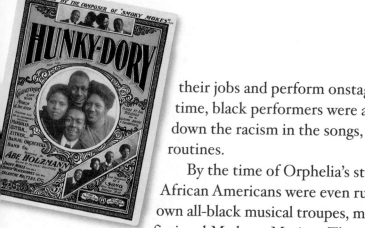

their jobs and perform onstage. Over time, black performers were able to tone down the racism in the songs, jokes, and routines.

By the time of Orphelia's story, a few African Americans were even running their own all-black musical troupes, much like the fictional Madame Meritta. These performers did not wear blackface or tattered clothing—they dressed like stars and became very popular with black audiences.

As Orphelia discovers, however, life on the road was far from glamorous. Troupes like Madame Meritta's performed in a different town each night, which meant many miles of hard travel. Although the performers wore elegant clothes and presented an image of luxury, few became rich. Most struggled to keep a band together and make a living, just as Madame Meritta and Mr. Othello do.

Some people, both black and white, disapproved of minstrel shows because they believed that nonreligious music—or, as Momma calls it, "sassy music"—was sinful. And most parents, even those who enjoyed minstrel music, didn't want their children becoming part of the rough life of show business.

As Orphelia's parents knew, black entertainers faced special dangers because of racism, particularly in the South.

Aida Overton Walker starred in a black-owned musical troupe.

When a minstrel show came to town, white citizens sometimes posted threatening signs warning the black performers to leave town as soon as the show was over.

Occasionally, racial hatred led to murder. A mob of whites might go after a black man and kill him, often by hanging. In some cases, these lynch mobs dragged black men right out of jail while white guards looked the other way, as happened to Uncle Winston. Unlike Uncle Winston, however, most victims of lynch mobs did not survive. Sadly, such crimes still occur. Today they are often called hate crimes.

By the turn of the century, America's industries were growing rapidly and needed workers. Thousands of black Southerners headed up the Mississippi River Valley to big cities such as Memphis, St. Louis, and Chicago. They brought with them the songs they had grown up with. Some of these songs were lively, toe-tapping folk songs. Others were slave songs or spirituals, also called *sorrow songs* because they expressed the suffering of slave life. As these musicians traveled, they traded songs and musical styles—and developed new ones.

Two new styles becoming especially popular at the time of Orphelia's story were blues and ragtime. Blues music

The Mississippi River Valley

162

tended to be slow and heartfelt, much like the religious slave spirituals, except that blues songs told of lost love and the troubles of everyday life. Great blues singers of the time, like Ma Rainey and Bessie Smith, could move their audiences to tears or make them jump with joy.

Ragtime had a very different feeling. It grew out of the lively folk music of southern blacks. Its strong, catchy rhythms had a slightly uneven, or *ragged,* beat.

Orphelia would likely have heard the "Maple Leaf Rag," a piano song written in Missouri by African American composer Scott Joplin. It became the first ragtime

As a young girl, Ma Rainey (second from right) toured in minstrel shows, where she sang her first blues songs. She later became known as the "Mother of the Blues."

hit and remains a favorite today.

Both ragtime and blues became popular across the country and were soon adopted by white musicians. Later these styles gave rise to other forms of American music that have become popular around the world— jazz, rock and roll, and more recently, rap.

In 1904, another new attraction that gained worldwide popularity was the St. Louis World's Fair. Seven times as big as Disneyland, the fair drew 20 million visitors in the eight months it

Sheet music for Scott Joplin's popular ragtime piano song

was open. Its grounds were filled with vast gardens and buildings the size of palaces, where visitors could view America's latest inventions as well as objects, animals, and even people from around the world. Fair-goers could watch a reenactment of a naval battle or stroll through a Japanese tea garden, an Irish castle, or a thatched Philippine village complete with native families—while enjoying brand-new treats such as the ice cream cone and Dr. Pepper. In the days before movies and television, the fair provided awestruck visitors with an astounding look at life around the globe. To a girl like Orphelia, the thrilling spectacle was beyond anything she could imagine.

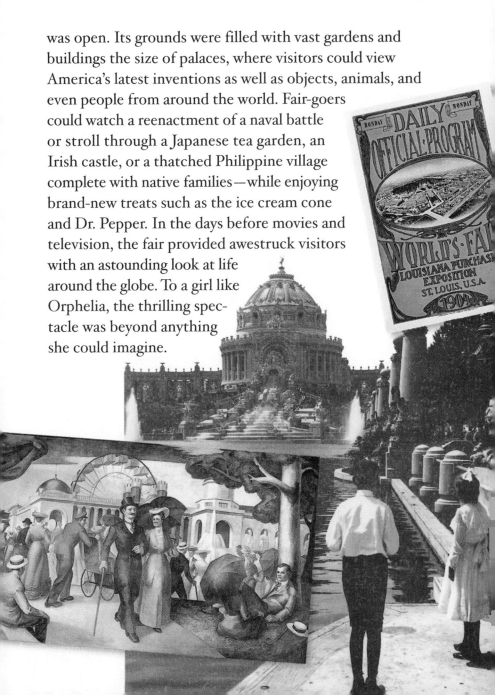

AUTHOR'S NOTE

In *The Minstrel's Melody,* my character Winston Taylor is nearly lynched after an incident in the Dixie Palace in 1892. My book is set in a real county—in fact, the county where I grew up—Lewis County in northeast Missouri. To my knowledge, and from what I've researched, I have not found any evidence that an actual lynching was reported in 1892 in Lewis County.

ABOUT THE AUTHOR

When Eleanora E. Tate was growing up in northeast Missouri, she loved to play piano and French horn, but her greatest love was books. At age twelve she decided to become a writer. Her first job was as news editor of a Des Moines, Iowa, weekly newspaper where she also wrote a music column called "blue lemons."

Eleanora Tate's books are *African American Musicians; The Secret of Gumbo Grove; A Blessing in Disguise; Don't Split the Pole; Thank You, Dr. Martin Luther King, Jr!; Front Porch Stories; Just an Overnight Guest;* and *Retold African Myths.* All of her books celebrate neighborhoods, communities, and the families who live there.

She and her husband, Zack Hamlett, III, live in Durham, North Carolina, where they enjoy jazz and blues concerts.